The Friendship Train of 1947 America's Christmas Gift to Europe

The Friendship Train of 1947
America's Christmas Gift to Europe

by

Linda Baten Johnson

The Friendship Train of 1947
America's Christmas Gift to Europe
By Linda Baten Johnson

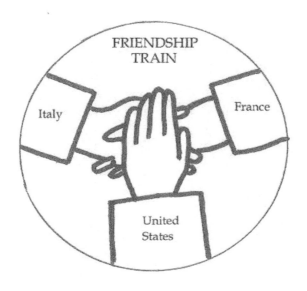

"Just as we know that you, our neighbors, would extend aid to us in time of crisis, we the American people, make this offering of food and friendship to you when your need for food is as great as the whole world's need for friendship."

--Sentiment taken from sticker placed on Friendship Train food boxes sent to France and Italy.

FRIENDSHIP TRAIN STOPS

From Los Angeles: Bakersfield, Fresno, Merced, Stockton, Oakland, and Sacramento (CA), Reno (NV), Ogden (UT), Green River, Rawlins, Laramie, and Cheyenne (WY), Sidney, North Platte, Kearney, Grand Island, Fremont and Omaha (NE), Council Bluffs, Boone, Ames, and Cedar Rapids (IA), Clinton, Sterling, and Chicago (IL).

North from Chicago: South Bend and Elkhart, (IN), Toledo, Cleveland, and Ashtabula (OH), Buffalo, Syracuse, Utica, Albany, and *New York City* (NY).

South from Chicago: Fort Wayne (IN), Mansfield (OH), Pittsburgh, Altoona, Lancaster, and Philadelphia (PA), Trenton (NJ), and *New York City* (NY).

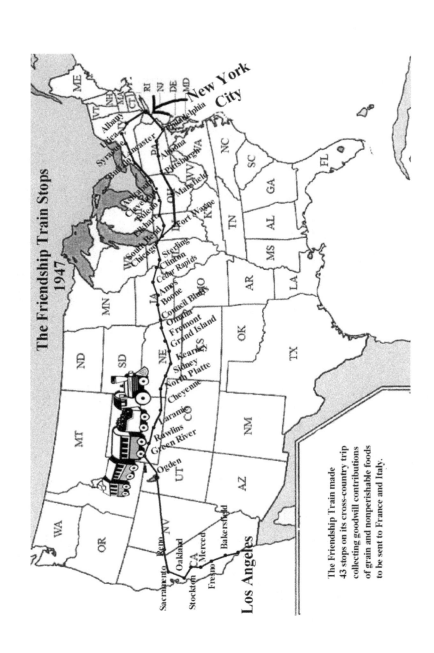

The Friendship Train Stops
1947

New York City

The Friendship Train made 43 stops on its cross-country trip collecting goodwill contributions of grain and nonperishable foods to be sent to France and Italy.

ONE

"How's your mama? "

If anyone else in eighth grade had dared ask, I'd have given him a black eye, but Billy and I are pals, and he knows almost everything about me. With me, that question's a problem. When kids want to be mean, they call me a bad luck charm, 'cause both my brothers died and my Mama's been acting a little crazy lately. So, I kept my mouth shut, stared at my scuffed shoes, and concentrated on the path ahead.

Billy Parker's been my best friend since he moved to California before the war. He gets picked on because he's short, kinda chubby, and has brown freckles sprinkled on his arms and face. Billy's dad works for the *Oakland Tribune*, and Mr. Parker told me straight out I'd have to be a fan of the New York Yankees to be welcome in their home. The man liked kidding me, but I adopted the Yankees to please him.

Billy shifted his arithmetic book to the other hand. "Those Brooklyn Bums sure scared me, but we got them in game seven. DiMaggio still your favorite player?"

"Yep." I pulled out my harmonica and played *Peg O' My Heart.* My playing had improved because people could name the songs without me telling them the titles. I slapped the harmonica on my sleeve to get the spit out.

"Jimmy, you know I didn't mean nothing by asking about your mama."

"I know. Truth is, she's no better." I returned the harmonica to my pocket. "Papa says Mama may have to go away."

"You have to go with her?"

"Don't know. I've got my chickens to tend, and I help Mrs. Martin sometimes." I twirled the hair in my cowlick, then whispered, "Mama doesn't know me anymore."

Billy heard me, but didn't say a word. He's a swell friend. He knows my mind is more on Mama than anything else these days.

"I wish she'd never gotten the letter." I muttered.

"The librarian sorta went off her head when she got the telegram about her husband getting killed on D-Day," Billy said. "But your mama seemed fine after you got the word about your brother."

"She was. She didn't start acting crazy until lately."

I like that Billy knows when to talk and when not to.

"All of us were cut up and blue about Johnny's death. I miss him something awful. He was working with me on my throwing." I rubbed my sleeve across my nose. "But Mama's a grown-up. She cried a lot at first, but she acted fine and dandy until August when the stupid old letter arrived, and the thing wasn't even in English."

"You're kidding."

"Nope. Mama took the letter to the French teacher at the high school to translate. Now Mama spends her days reading the thing over and over and over."

Billy bumped my shoulder with his. "Guess you got it memorized, huh?"

"Sure do, but when I get home, Mama will tell me what this nice family in France said about my brother Johnny — like I ain't heard it a million times. Then she'll start in on how we need to give them food."

I kicked a pebble toward Billy, who shuffle stepped, and aimed the pebble back. He gave our makeshift ball a big kick when we got to the turn to his house.

"See you tomorrow, and don't take any wooden nickels." He wagged his pointer finger to emphasize each word.

He gave the same advice every day, and I responded with a snappy farewell salute. The closer I got to home, the slower I walked. I picked up a stick, mimicked DiMaggio's wide stance, and swung for the fences. I almost fell watching my imaginary homerun soar into the bleachers when my foot caught in a washed-out spot on the path. I'd tripped in the same place Tuesday, so I knocked some loose gravel in the hole. Maybe Billy and I would fix it Saturday. Didn't want to fall and break my leg. If that happened, I couldn't keep up with baseball practice. I wrote "fix hole" on my arithmetic book cover.

I stopped by the rosebushes. A light glowing from our kitchen startled me 'cause Mama sorta lived in the dark now and Papa didn't get home from the rail yard till six. Through the window, Mama looked peaceful. Her hair was combed, she wore an ironed dress, and she had a small wash pan on her lap. She began singing *Marching to Zion* as she peeled potatoes, dug out the bad spots and dropped them into the pan. She finished three potatoes before I backed away.

Mama looked normal, but I hadn't seen her eyes. I paced back and forth between the rosebushes and the path. Home had been different since we'd received the letter. Most days, her hair would look a mess and she'd be wearing a wrinkled dirty housecoat, and she certainly hadn't done much cooking for us lately.

My stomach turned cartwheels. I covered my mouth and told myself not to puke. After the sick feeling passed, I looked at the gray sky and decided to say an insurance prayer.

"God, I wish Mama could be like she used to be." I paused, remembering something the minister always said about God's plans and our plans. "Now God, I know You have Your own plans, but it would be real nice for me and Papa if You . . . if You . . . oh, Thy will be done. Amen."

When I finished, I saw Papa striding up the path to our house. I wanted to bury my face against his wide, strong body, feel his rough scratchy overalls against my skin, and inhale his familiar smell of railroad grease and Old Spice aftershave. I imagined Papa wrapping me in his arms and squeezing me, but I'd turned 13 this month, so I waited for him by the front gate and tried to look nonchalant.

"You're home early, Papa."

"That I am." He patted my back. "I asked someone to cover for me so we could talk. I swear you're having a growth spurt. Pretty soon, you'll be resting your arm on my shoulder." He motioned to the front porch and we sat.

Papa put his lunch pail down next to him, pulled out his pocketknife and started cleaning the grease from under his nails. Papa always started on the left hand first. I settled in, my shoulder leaning against his arm.

We listened to Mrs. Martin's radio blare an advertisement about little liver pills. She didn't like wearing her hearing aids, so the whole block heard her programs. Across the street, the Wosnik kids threw a stick for their cocker spaniel to fetch.

I sneaked a sidelong glance at my father. Papa's mustache turned up slightly on the ends, making his face look happy. He had broad shoulders, big muscles, black, wavy hair, and dark eyes, and I always wanted to look like him.

When I was little, I'd told Papa about my wish, and he'd laughed, tousled my dishwater-brown hair and said my blue eyes would never turn brown, and I'd probably grow up to look like Jimmy Stewart from the pictures. Papa predicted I'd be tall, skinny, and all angles. He told me my long arms were perfect for catching those hard-to-reach fly balls which made me feel better, but I secretly hoped Papa might be wrong about my looks.

"Talked to Doc Armstrong about your mama." Papa slipped the knife into his pocket. "He thinks a scenery change might help Ida get past this rough patch." Papa watched Mrs. Martin sweeping her front porch instead of looking at me. "Your Aunt Sue wants your mama with her in Los Angeles for a month or two."

"What about me?"

"Think we can handle the cooking and cleaning back here?" Papa now studied the kids and their feisty dog across the street.

"Sure. I can pack your lunches, and I know how to make scrambled eggs."

"Going to mention the trip to Ida at dinner. You never know how your mama will take things. We don't want any more flying spaghetti." Papa tried to laugh, but it came out more like a three-part cough. "You've grown a lot lately, and Mama's mind seems to be stuck in the past right now. Doc thinks that might be why she doesn't know you all the time."

That didn't make sense. How could she forget me? Ever?

Papa slapped my leg. "Better face the music."

"Yeah. My chickens are probably wondering where their dinner is." I scooted inside to my room to change while Papa headed for the kitchen.

"My pretty, pretty Ida." Papa gave a wolf whistle.

"You always think I look pretty when I'm in the kitchen." Mama laughed.

"You know the way to a man's heart, Sweetie, and you've got two hungry men here."

I hung up my school clothes and listened to my parents.

"Wow!" Papa said. "You expecting an army? You must have peeled 20 potatoes."

"Not an army, just a few extra. Robert, I got the nicest letter from a French family. They hid our Johnny during the war, so I invited them to dinner. Let me read you the letter."

"Oh, Ida, France is a long way for them to come." Papa spoke softer, sounded sadder.

I knew Mama would be fumbling for the letter, and she began the story she repeated every single night.

"Their name is Deschamps. Isn't the name pretty and musical-sounding? Our Johnny parachuted into their farm, and they saved him from the Germans. They hid our boy in a haystack and cared for him until he went back to his unit. Now, the Deschamps need our help, Robert. They need food."

"Sweetie, you read that letter to me yesterday."

"I did?"

"Yes, you did."

7

"Did I tell you their land was destroyed by the war and now the weather's been horrible and they can't grow anything?"

"You told me," Papa said tenderly. "I'll wash up, and we can figure out what to do with all these potatoes." Papa kept talking without taking a breath. "We can mash some for dinner and use leftovers for your potato pancakes. You can make potato soup. I love your soup in my thermos, and maybe we can fry some for breakfast."

"We have enough food to share. Are you sure the Deschamps won't come?" Mama's words sounded like a moan.

"Sweetie, they're not coming."

The chicken coop sat behind the house, but instead of going through the kitchen, I dashed out the front door. I glimpsed Papa holding Mama in his arms, and they swayed back and forth like they were dancing. Before I even filled the bucket with chicken feed, my eyes started to water. I must have gotten some cinders in them. Living close to the railroad, you never know when you might get cinders in your eyes.

I found eight eggs, so now I had a dozen to sell. Maybe I'd treat Billy to the Abbott and Costello movie this weekend. They made me laugh, and I could use a couple of yucks.

Mama eyed me suspiciously when I washed the eggs, but she didn't say anything. She filled three plates and Papa said the blessing. I kept quiet and concentrated on the mashed potatoes and fried Spam, dreading what I knew might come next.

Most nights Mama observed me anxiously, then yelled for Papa to make me leave. I didn't understand why she always knew Papa, but not me. The spaghetti sauce stain on the wall from two nights ago looked like a puffy red cloud floating above the stove clock. She'd thrown my plate at the wall, saying she wouldn't feed her spaghetti to strays. Her anger scared me. The mama I knew fed any hobo with a sad story who knocked on the door, even if she didn't know him.

"We should have waited on our children. Where are they? And who is he?" Mama pointed her finger straight at me.

"Ida, our daughter Martha is a grown woman with twin boys, Caleb and Joshua. They're almost two." Papa patted Mama's hand.

"And our boys?" Her voice rose in pitch.

"Johnny died in the war. The fever took our Andrew in '43, and this is James, our Jimmy, sitting right here. Growing like a weed, isn't he? He really shot up this year." Papa nodded in my direction.

Mama fixed her eyes on me with skepticism. I pushed the potatoes around on my plate, made mountains, and smashed them down. I waited for the explosion, but the upheaval didn't come, and Mama's mind returned to its favorite track.

"Robert, I got the nicest letter from . . ."

Papa held his palm toward Mama. "Ida, how would you like to visit your sister in Los Angeles?"

"Sue? Really? I'd love to. When?"

Papa's shoulders relaxed. "In a few weeks. I've got some time coming in November. Maybe we'll see real live movie stars."

"I'd like to see Maureen O'Hara. The papers say she has beautiful red hair." Mama ran her fingers through her own reddish hair.

"For my money, yours is prettier." Papa picked up the newspaper and tapped it on the edge of the table. "Jimmy, you've rearranged those potatoes enough. Eat them and give your mama a hand clearing the table."

Each night, Papa read aloud from the newspaper while Mama did dishes and I worked on homework. Listening to the stories kept Mama calm, and Papa often read until my bedtime.

"Here's the Drew Pearson column everyone's talking about." Papa folded the paper in half.

"Is he the man who does the news on Sunday?" I asked.

"The very same. He keeps an eye on the politicians in Washington and makes sure they're doing what they should."

"What's he say?" Mama placed a plate in the dish rack.

"He proposes running a train from California to New York to collect food from ordinary Americans to give to the starving people in Europe."

"That would mean France." Mama interrupted.

"That would mean France," Papa said. "Pearson says the Russian commies gave the Europeans a few

10

carloads of wheat, and now those countries are leaning toward communism. He believes food donations from Americans will save lives and keep the Europeans from changing their government."

"We could send food to the family that helped Johnny." Mama wiped her hands on a dish towel. "I can't remember their name, but I have the letter here." Mama retrieved the worn folded paper from her apron pocket.

Papa patted the sofa. "Come sit with us, Ida. I'll read the whole thing."

Mama sat next to me and listened to Papa reading. When I stood to go to bed, Mama kissed her fingers and placed them on my cheek.

"Night, Jimmy," she said.

Mama had called me by name. I replayed Mama's two words in my head while I brushed my teeth, put on my pajamas, and snuggled under the covers. She'd known me. She'd called me Jimmy. I went to bed happy, not realizing Drew Pearson's newspaper column would change our lives forever.

TWO

Mama changed. One day, warm oatmeal cookies waited when I got home from school. Clean clothes filled my closet, and Mama had even replaced the button on my favorite plaid shirt. After dinner, Mama harmonized with the radio while she washed the dishes.

Each night Papa told us about names submitted for Pearson's train which included a Train of Grain, a Good Will Train, the Feed'em Train, and America's Train—so they'd know the food was from us and not the commies. Finally, "Friendship Train" became the official name for the coast-to-coast food collection for our European friends in need.

One newspaper editor said this humanitarian effort would have no government involvement, because ordinary people could get the job done before Congress could put together a committee. Mama and Papa both laughed, so I did too. Our family felt normal, until Mama's announcement.

"I can't wait any longer," Mama said and handed Papa a Prince Albert tobacco can. "Look inside."

Papa opened the tin, pulled out a wad of money, and whistled. The bills had a tobacco smell, and I felt my eyes widen at the sight.

"Ida, how much money's in here?"

"Count it." Mama smiled.

I saw tens, twenties, even a fifty! My mouth fell open, and I stood to get a better look at Mama's wealth. The mirror over the radio reflected my gaping mouth and bulging eyes, so I snapped my mouth shut and rubbed my chin like people do when they think serious thoughts. I didn't have the foggiest idea how Mama got so much money. I'd read about buried pirate treasure and about loot stashed by bank robbers, but Mama and bad guys didn't fit together.

"My count is—" Papa whispered in Mama's ear after he finished stacking the bills.

"That's right." Mama glowed.

"Where did this money come from?"

"The government sent us a check after Johnny died in France, plus some back pay."

"When? Our Johnny died in '45. This is '47. And how did you get the cash?" Papa stuttered his questions.

"The check came a few months after he died," Mama said.

Papa fingered the bills on the nearest stack. I wish he hadn't whispered the amount, because I sure wanted to know how much money we had on the coffee table. Papa's shoulders slumped, and he stared at the money like it was a snake coiled to strike. His jaw worked, and I could tell he was trying to say something.

"The bank account's in my name, Ida. I give you cash each month for the house budget. If this money came in a check, how did you get these bills?" Papa rubbed his temples like he had a bad headache.

"I took the check to the bank and asked Annie Kidd if she could cash it. Annie sings in the choir with me, and when she saw what it was, she gave me the money. Aren't you pleased?"

Papa did not look pleased, but all those greenbacks lined up like soldiers sure tickled me. Maybe this Christmas I'd get the Louisville Slugger bat I hadn't gotten for my birthday earlier this month, and I'd probably get a really good outfielder's glove. I flexed the fingers on my left hand, and then pounded my right fist again and again into my left palm, planning how I'd oil my new glove, loosen the leather, and soften the pocket.

"Why?" Papa's one word spoke shock, hurt, anger, and disbelief.

I quit shaping my pretend glove and let my hands rest. As my hands stilled, Mama's started to move. She washed her hands over and over with invisible soap, something she did when worried.

"Well, you know the expression 'he bought the farm', and how the awful saying meant a family got a house because someone died in the war?"

Papa held out his hands, asking for more information.

"We've been saving for a home for years, but I didn't want this money to go toward a house, a house bought with Johnny's blood." Mama finished quietly.

"Couldn't you trust me to understand that?" Papa breathed loudly, his mouth open.

I did not belong in this discussion. I got up to leave, but Papa put out a hand, blocked my exit, and gently pushed me back into the chair. He stared at our Zenith like he'd never seen a radio before. No one spoke, and I started counting the clock's pendulum swings for something to do. I'd reached the number 32, when Mama knelt and put her hand on Papa's knee.

"Robert, Drew Pearson's train is our answer."

"Ida, why didn't you tell me about the check?"

"I was afraid."

"Of what? I've been struggling to make ends meet for this family, and you've had this money secreted away."

Papa's voice made me shiver.

"Robert, not telling you has been burning a hole in my heart." Mama moved her fingers across the coarse material on the knee of Papa's pants.

Papa continued to study the radio case, and he found the Zenith so fascinating I started looking at it too. Papa didn't look at Mama or at me.

Since he wasn't talking, and I definitely wasn't talking, Mama picked up where she left off. "That column by Drew Pearson showed me how we can get Johnny's money to the Deschamps. They sent us

15

Christmas cards for the past two years, but they never asked for anything until this letter came in August."

She held out the tattered letter, which Papa ignored. He continued his examination of the Zenith.

"Robert, I've been crazy with worry since we got this letter telling us that they didn't have any food. I knew we had to help them, but I didn't know how."

"That's not the issue." Papa motioned for Mama to get up.

"I should have told you about the money, but last night, everything suddenly became clear," Mama said.

"Oh?" Papa's words sounded cold.

"They'll need railroad men, Robert. You could be on the Friendship Train crew. You could make sure this money gets to Henri and Sophie Deschamps."

Papa shook his head in frustration. "How could I leave you and Jimmy?"

Tears snaked down Mama's cheeks, and she put her fingers on Papa's lips, but his words kept tumbling out.

"Ida, I've been worried sick about you. With losing both Andrew and Johnny, I figured the grief crushed you. I thought you were having a nervous breakdown, and so did Doc Armstrong."

"Everything got mixed up after the letter came. I couldn't think."

"And Jimmy?" Papa tilted his head toward me. "You acted like you didn't even know our boy."

I scrunched down in the chair to make myself smaller. I didn't want them to talk about me.

Mama lifted her hands in a helpless gesture. "I wasn't myself. I couldn't think of anything except the money and the Deschamps family. Robert, I talked to the Deschamps, and they talked to me. I asked them to share our food."

Mama had talked to them, a lot. I'd heard her, even though I pretended not to. She chatted about recipes, about the weather, about Johnny, and she spoke aloud for herself and for the French family. I don't know if Papa knew. I sure never told him.

"You've got a big heart, Ida,"

Mama smiled. "Then you'll do it, you'll go on the Friendship Train."

"Sweetie, we don't keep secrets from each other," Papa said firmly.

I'd never heard my parents argue. But this seemed like a fight—like two different fights with Mama fretting about feeding the Deschamps, and Papa questioning her trust in him. I closed my eyes, crossed the fingers on both hands, and wished my chair would be like Jonah's whale and swallow me up and spit me out in my room. Maybe the double cross ruined the wish, 'cause nothing happened.

"Robert, I'll write a letter to Drew Pearson asking if you can work on the Friendship Train, and then the French teacher can write to the Deschamps."

Papa cocked his head. "Good plan. I'll hop on the Friendship Train with Drew Pearson, say hello to Governor Earl Warren, pay my respects to Harry Warner, the film mogul who's helping Pearson, and maybe chat with Ronald Reagan, who's lining up movie stars to participate."

The chill in Papa's voice made me fidgety. I'd never heard him talk that way to Mama before. I thought about trying to leave again, but I didn't want to upset Papa any more than he already was.

"Robert, you'll get to go," Mama said. "I sensed you would when you were reading Drew Pearson's column."

Mama sounded so confident, she convinced me Papa would soon be traveling across the country with the world-famous Mr. Pearson.

"And how would you pay the rent and buy groceries?"

"We've got savings and a little extra money hidden in the glass chicken on the top shelf." Mama looked at Papa for an approval he didn't give.

Papa stuffed the money back in the can and stood. "I'm going to Minnie's Café and get a cup of coffee. Jimmy, you better hit the sack."

"I can make you some coffee." Mama reached for Papa, but he didn't meet her eyes.

"I need the air," Papa said.

I mumbled goodnight and headed to what my parents called the boys' room, even though I was the only boy left alive in our family. My room felt awfully lonely.

"Jimmy, Jimmy, wake up." Papa shook my shoulders.

I rubbed my eyes, squinted at the window and saw nothing but darkness.

"Your mama's not in the house, and there's no note. You know where she is?"

My parents called me a sleepyhead for good reason. I struggled to open my eyes.

"Jimmy, answer me. Did Mama tell you where she was going?" Papa demanded my attention.

"No, I went to bed after you left."

"Did you hear anything? Did anyone stop by? Did your mama come in to say good night?" Papa asked too many questions.

"No. What's wrong?" I squinted, trying to bring Papa's face into focus.

"Get dressed. I'll put the coffee on," Papa said.

Papa knew I didn't drink coffee, but by the time I'd laced my shoes, the strong aroma floated from the kitchen. I stumbled to my chair, and Papa put down his steaming mug and poured coffee for me.

"I'm going to your sister's place. If Martha needed help with the twins, even at midnight, your mama would have gone."

I nodded and checked the clock. *Jeez Louise*, I thought, *it's two in the morning.*

"You stay here. When Mama comes in, tell her I'm sorry. Tell her I'll do my best to get on the Friendship Train and get her money to the Deschamps." I nodded

19

and squinted at the clock. The little hand did point to two.

"You know, Jimmy, if you mix your coffee with milk, you might like it." Papa slid a milk bottle toward me and hurried out the kitchen door.

After Papa left, I had my first cup of coffee. I tried it black like my parents drank their coffee and decided mine needed some milk. I checked the clock again. Where could Mama be? Why would she go out in the middle of the night? She didn't even like going out at night without Papa.

I took my time drinking the coffee and blew on the light tan liquid before each sip while I worried about Mama. I'd just choked down my last swallow, when Papa yelled.

"Jimmy, open the door."

I knocked over Papa's coffee in my rush.

Papa carried Mama like a rag doll, her motionless head rested in the crook of Papa's arm. The blood on her head mingled with her red hair. Papa moved quickly, but Mama didn't move at all. Her pale face paralyzed me.

"Get the bedroom door, then run to Doc Armstrong's," Papa ordered, "and pound on his door till you wake him. Tell him it's an emergency."

I stared at Mama. My feet wouldn't move.

"The bedroom door," Papa said again.

I opened their door, and Papa placed Mama gently on the brown and navy quilt she'd made for him last Christmas.

"Is she okay?"

I stepped toward the bed, but Papa pointed to the front door.

"Run, Jimmy! Get Doc Armstrong. Wake him up. Make him come with you."

I raced through the darkened streets, remembering Mama's unmoving body and Papa's frightened face. I did what Papa told me. I ran. I ran as fast as I could, but I wasn't fast enough.

THREE

For the next two days, ladies with casseroles paraded in and out of our kitchen. Martha left the twins with her mother-in-law and took over our house. Martha and I stood eye to eye now, but she wouldn't be growing any taller. She looked like Papa. She got Papa's dark hair, dark eyes, stocky shape, and his energy. She became a whirlwind of activities and she cleaned, cooked, hovered over me and Papa, and chatted with every person who showed up.

Martha repeated the same story to every person — Mama had gone out for a walk, stepped in a hole, fell and hit her head on a rock which killed her instantly. According to Doc Armstrong, Mama would have lived had she been taller or shorter, or if she had slipped and broken her fall, or if she had taken a different path, or if the moon had been brighter and she could have seen the path. Or, or, or. But no "ors" happened.

Neighbors murmured "What a terrible tragedy," "What a horrible accident," "Please call if you need help," and "You must all be in shock."

Martha wrote the name of every dessert, flower, or food dish and who brought it on a tablet so we could write thank-you notes. She agreed when they murmured we'd been blessed by Mama's quick passing. I hated when either the casserole ladies or Martha said Mama's death was a blessing. I guess they meant not suffering was the blessing, but I sure didn't feel blessed. Maybe I was bad luck, like the kids said. I'd probably caused Mama's death by not filling in that hole. I'd known about it and hadn't done anything about it. I didn't hang around the kitchen much, because I didn't want those women clucking and cooing over me.

My Sunday school teacher stopped by and told me that God loved and cared for me, but I wondered about that. If God did love me, why did he take Mama away? Maybe God didn't love me. Maybe God was punishing me for not fixing the hole in the path. Nobody stopping by our house would have offered me any sympathy if they'd known I'd caused Mama's death.

I didn't know for certain that Mama caught her foot in the hole I'd tripped on, and I'd asked myself a million times the past two days why I hadn't fixed it. I'd filled the hole the morning after Mama died, but my repair didn't matter, because now our kitchen table and counters were piled high with funeral food. Nothing looked good to me, and I didn't think I'd be able to eat until I cleared my conscience by telling Papa the truth, but his sadness terrified me.

Papa spent his time alone in the bedroom. When people asked about him, Martha said Papa needed rest, but he didn't look rested when he came out. Actually, he only came out when Martha insisted. His puffy red eyes looked hollow and his sagging body reminded me of a balloon without any air. Papa and I both stayed in our rooms. Papa was a prisoner of grief and me of guilt.

Toward dinner time on the second day, Mrs. Martin brought her banana pudding and asked Martha to call me. Without her hearing aids, Mrs. Martin spoke loudly, so I heard her plain as day and came right out. Our neighbor swept me into a talcum powder and lavender embrace and then held both my shoulders while she talked to me.

"Jimmy, I know how you like banana pudding." Mrs. Martin shouted. "I wanted to make something special, you dear boy. The pudding came to my mind. I hope you enjoy every bite." Mrs. Martin pointed to the round bowl topped with circles of wafers and bananas.

"Yes ma'am, I do love your banana pudding." I shouted to her. "Mama says, uh Mama always said that you were famous for it. Thank you."

Mrs. Martin pulled me in for another hug, gave Martha's hand a pat, and marched out the front door. Martha reached for the tablet to write down banana pudding and Mrs. Martin's name. Then she started to giggle. Martha's too serious a person to giggle, but she giggled until tears came to her eyes. I stared at her, wondering if she'd lost her mind.

She tried to make her face serious and closed her mouth, but a loud snort and cackle broke out.

Grinning, Martha held out her arms to me and bellowed, "Jimmy, I know how you like banana pudding."

I stared at her. Should I go find Dr. Armstrong?

"Jimmy, you dear boy." Martha stretched her arms toward me. "Jimmy, I know you like banana pudding."

Then I caught Martha's silliness, rubbed my tummy, and yelled right back at her. "Yes ma'am, I do. I do *love* banana pudding."

I ran to Martha for a big hug, and then went to the other side of the kitchen, and Martha started the routine again.

Our act became more hilarious each time we repeated it. By the fourth time, we both held our sides, and tears of laughter spilled down our cheeks.

Papa.

"What's going on in here?" Papa demanded.

Martha bit her bottom lip and started to explain, then she looked at me and we both burst out laughing. We couldn't explain to Papa why my liking banana pudding struck us so funny. He gave us a puzzled look, shook his head, and went back to the bedroom. Martha and I tried not to look at each other, but then one of us would giggle or cough or sniff, and we were laughing our heads off again. We finally quit when our stomachs hurt too much to laugh any more and Papa came back into the kitchen, still mystified by our behavior.

Martha dished up big bowls of Mrs. Martin's banana pudding. I had told our neighbor the truth; I did love her banana pudding. I licked the last bit off my spoon and handed my bowl to Martha, my grown-up sister who'd acted like a goofy kid with me tonight.

I don't know much about life, the kind Mama and Papa shared, but I knew any time Martha or I ate banana pudding, whether together or apart, we'd think about each other and our laughter in the kitchen that night.

Papa poured a glass of milk and grabbed the shoe shine box from the broom closet.

"Jimmy, go get your Sunday shoes and mine. They'll need a shining." Papa spread newspaper on the kitchen table and set out the brown and black polish, the rags, the brush, and the buffing cloth.

"I'll get Mama's shoes too, and then I'm leaving," Martha said, "but I'll be back first thing in the morning."

A baseball size lump choked me. Truth time. After Martha left, I'd tell Papa about causing Mama's death. What would he say? Would he kick me out of the house? Well, nothing could be worse than this gnawing in my gut. I had to tell Papa the truth. I took the laces from my shoes and Papa's, pulled the tongues up, and wiped the dust off. I practiced in my head. *I'm to blame for Mama's death. No. Mama's fall wasn't really an accident. No. I caused Mama's death. No.* Nothing sounded right. Poor Papa, would he hate me forever?

"Here you go." Martha came back with Mama's shoes. "I'll be here before eight. The appointment's at nine, right?"

Papa nodded to her and she left. He worried the scratches right off the shoes with paste, then passed them to me. We had a system because we polished shoes together every Saturday.

"Papa, about Mama's fall." I gazed at the shoes. I didn't want to see his face when he heard what I'd done, or rather not done.

"You did a good job on the right. Now work on this one." Papa handed me his left shoe.

"I walk the path where she fell every day going and coming from school." I tried again.

"Do you have a clean white shirt? If you don't, you need to let Martha know tomorrow." Papa now held Mama's shoe, and he rubbed in the polish, examining every crevice.

"Martha got out a white shirt for me, brushed my jacket too." I put my feet in my shoes and Papa used the buffing rag to finish mine, then he put his shoes on and handed me the cloth.

"Done," Papa said. "Better get some rest. Tomorrow will be a long day."

"But I need to tell you . . ."

"Later." Papa held his shoes with the right fingers and Mama's with his left, and pushed down the light switch with his elbow. "Don't forget to brush your teeth."

I couldn't sleep and welcomed the morning, then I remembered what today meant. When we entered the Dixon Funeral Home, I reached for Papa's hand. He squeezed my hand and didn't let go the whole morning. Martha carried Mama's dark green Sunday dress, her freshly-polished black high heels, her pearls, and a lace-edged handkerchief. We picked a casket with cream-colored insides to show off Mama's reddish hair.

Our minister met us there and asked questions about Bible verses, Mama's favorite things, and songs she might want sung. I told him about hearing her sing *Marching to Zion* before she died. He said the hymn would be a good one for the choir to sing, and he suggested Annie Kidd sing *The Lord's Prayer* to close the service.

I've been to several funerals other than those for my two brothers. In our neighborhood, when anyone died, you paid your respects. But funerals raised a lot of questions. I'd discussed some of those with Billy, but he didn't have any answers either. We wondered why they put glasses on a dead person, and why the people in caskets at Dixon's always had redder cheeks than those at Speckman's Funeral Home. Why did flowers smell different at a funeral? Why did the deceased hold something, like a handkerchief or Bible? Could the people in the casket hear the nice things being said about them or the songs being sung? I kept those questions to myself, because everyone acted business-like and formal.

Mama's funeral and burial didn't take long. I'd dreaded the service, thinking it would take forever and that I wouldn't be able to stand it. Instead, Papa and I had the house to ourselves by Sunday evening, and we polished off the meatloaf and the lime Jell-O mixed up with cottage cheese and pineapple. I washed dishes while Papa wrote short notes to the funeral-food ladies and taped the papers in the clean dishes.

"Papa, you worried about going back to work?"

"Probably feel strange. You worried about school?"

"Kids forget after a few days."

"Same with adults." Papa sighed and pushed the thank-you notes aside. "Jimmy, you know your mother and I loved each other, but we did disagree, sometimes."

"I know." I put the dish towel on the back door rack.

"Your mother must have gone out looking for me. We couldn't stand to let a quarrel simmer." Papa's breathing sounded heavy. "She's walked that path a million times. I can't imagine what happened."

"I can!" The words rushed out. "It's all my fault. I noticed a hole in the path, but I didn't fill it."

I couldn't breathe. I gulped and gasped for air, waiting for Papa to tell me to leave, that he never wanted to see me again.

Papa's arms surrounded me. "No, Jimmy, no. It is not your fault. God decided to take her home. She'd completed her time here on earth."

Papa rocked me back and forth, the way he'd done with Mama in the kitchen that night. He rocked me until my sobs stopped and I was still. I rested my head against Papa's chest and listened to the steady beat of his heart.

"I don't understand why God would take Mama away." I leaned back so I could see his face.

"Neither do I." Papa smoothed my hair and led me to the living room. We sat on the sofa together.

"Papa, I fixed the hole. Nobody will ever trip there again. I did a good job."

"I'm sure you did, Jimmy."

"You don't hate me?"

He took my chin between his thumb and fingers and made me look him in the eye. "Mama's dying was not your fault. The good book says nobody knows how long their time on earth will be. We must be thankful for her life."

"I am, but I'm going to miss her."

"Me too." Papa handed me his handkerchief.

I wiped my eyes, then blew my nose three times and returned it to Papa.

Papa gave a half chuckle. "Don't think I'll put that back in my pocket." He placed the used handkerchief on the coffee table and checked his watch. "Six o'clock on a Sunday night. Let's see what Drew Pearson has to say."

I had a lot more questions about God, but instead of asking, I fussed with the radio dial.

Papa leaned back in his chair. "I wrote Mr. Pearson like your mama wanted. I told the man that you and I would like to ride his Friendship Train. I doubt we'll hear from him, but I did write the letter. Felt I owed her that much."

We listened to the broadcast in silence. Midway through the program, Mr. Pearson announced the Association of American Railroads was putting a freight train a mile long at the committee's disposal. He challenged listeners to contact local churches or service clubs about making food donations.

"Papa,"

"Yes, listen."

After the commercial for Lee Hats, Pearson talked about helping neighbors and answering this call for help from Europe with grain, not guns. He called the train a covered wagon in reverse — pioneering this time not for gold, but for the Golden Rule. He said the train would leave Los Angeles November 7 with five boxcars and more would be added on the route across our nation.

I wished Mama could have heard Mr. Pearson with us, and maybe she did. In my opinion, angels do pretty much anything they please, and my mama's angel stayed very busy the next few weeks.

FOUR

On my first day back in school, Billy never left my side. Students whispered comments behind cupped hands and parted for us like the Red Sea parted for Moses. Billy chattered about everything from President Truman down to his mother's latest sewing project—bibbed aprons. I liked Billy because he knew when not to talk, but that day I liked him for filling the empty spaces with words.

At ten o'clock we assembled in the cafeteria, which doubled as an auditorium complete with a stage. Margaret Allen marched between Billy and me. The three of us had been in the same class for the past four years, and Billy and I made up a new nickname for her each school term. This year, we called her Giant or Dragon because she'd grown taller than anyone in our class, including Miss Rhodes, and she breathed loudly through her nose when we annoyed her.

Billy stepped on Margaret's shoe heel—by accident—and she almost tripped over me when I suddenly stopped to tie my shoes. She glared at us and inhaled and exhaled noisily. Billy and I thought her nose-breathing routine would prepare her to become a full-fledged, fire-breathing dragon by adulthood. We encouraged her practice every day.

Since the babies in first and second grades fidgeted in assemblies, Principal Collins kept full school gatherings short. His black-rimmed glasses made his gray eyes look bigger than normal, and they seemed to know just what you were thinking when he saw you in the classroom, the hall or in his office. I'd been to the principal's office more than once, usually with Billy over some prank we'd pulled.

Today, Mr. Collins wore his brown plaid jacket and a starched white shirt with a tight brown tie to squeeze his thick neck. His body shape reminded me of Humpty Dumpty from the baby books. He limped because he caught a bullet in the leg when he fought in Europe. Papa said war changed Walter Collins, but I don't remember him from before, so I can't say.

What I can say is that our principal could match a revival preacher when he had a good head of steam, and he started strong this morning. He covered the stage, shoes pounding the floor with an alternating clump thump, clump thump, and he didn't need the microphone.

"America fought a great war to stop Hitler and to free Europe, but the danger remains. The danger is hunger, and the danger is communism. You," he pointed to our class, "and you," he indicated the fifth graders, "and even you," he pointed straight at the big-eyed first graders, "can help feed European children and defeat the Communists."

Principal Collins used to teach history, so we weren't surprised that he had a world map on an easel on the stage. "The Friendship Train will stop here in Oakland before crossing the United States." He moved a pointer from our city to the east coast. In New York City, the food will be transferred from train cars to ships and sent to France and Italy." He pointed to those countries for the kids who didn't know France or Italy from a hole in the ground.

I always started with the boot-shaped country of Italy when we labeled world maps with countries and capitals in geography class. I reached behind Margaret and tapped Billy's shoulder. I mouthed "Italy" to him. Billy gave me his goofiest look and answered a voiceless "Really?" We both made A's in geography. Margaret glared at me, then Billy. This was a pretty good day. We'd made her mad twice already.

Principal Collins sensed the little ones were getting restless, and he cranked the performance up a notch. He showed us a plate with a tiny piece of meat, bread, a few potatoes, and four carrots. He must have taped the food to the plate because he tilted the plate so everyone could see, and the food didn't splat on the floor.

"Look at this plate," Mr. Collins commanded. "Study it. Think about it. This is what a European child your age eats—in a week. Yes, you heard right, a whole week. In America, most children eat this much food every day, usually more."

I stared at the half-empty plate and remembered the chicken casserole we ate last night and the eggs and toast we had this morning. Macaroni and cheese and apple pie aromas drifted from the cafeteria kitchen and reminded us we'd soon be eating another meal. Everyone studied the plate.

"The children in Europe don't have much food. Some don't even have families. The orphanages house children whose parents died during the war years. Those poor kids don't need toys for Christmas. No, they don't need toys. They need food, and I know the students at this school will make sure they get fed."

Mr. Collins had us thinking, from the first graders to the big kids. The auditorium was quiet.

"This," Principal Collins waved a newspaper like a flagger for the train, "is how you and I can help. We can fill boxcars with food to give to the starving people in Europe. Listen to what journalist Drew Pearson says:

'I am sure that the original Friendship Train starting at Los Angeles with one boxcar to hold the sacks of flour and bags of wheat donated by the people of each city would add new boxcars at San Francisco, Sacramento, Reno, Salt Lake City, Cheyenne, Denver and Omaha until it became a great rolling tribute from the heart of America rumbling across the continent to New York and thence to Europe.

35

This would convince the people of Europe that this food comes not from the United States government, as a part of its foreign policy, but from every dinner table in America.'"

Our principal put the newspaper down by the measly food plate. "I've seen whole towns destroyed by bombs and by the Germans. The soil suffered from the war, and the bad weather destroyed any hope for decent crops this year. If we don't give, communism will take over Europe. The train is coming through our city on November the 8th. Who will help fill a Friendship Train boxcar with food?"

Some teachers said, "Yes" and "We will" and applauded.

Mr. Collins tried again. "Can you help defeat communism in Europe?"

This time the bigger kids yelled "Yes" and "You bet" because they knew they wouldn't get in trouble.

"Do you want to give food to a poor starving child?"

He got a rousing response from almost everybody, but I noticed three first graders sniffling and rubbing their eyes with tiny fists. Margaret Allen's baby sister sucked her thumb so hard her cheeks disappeared into deep holes. She looked at Margaret for reassurance, and our dragon-breathing classmate gave her sister a comforting smile.

By the time we headed to our classrooms, we'd vowed to fill a Friendship Train boxcar with evaporated milk. *Good grief.* Those people who cheered and committed to fill a boxcar must not know how huge a boxcar is. Papa let me get inside one last summer, so I understood the size difference, and a boxcar is very big and an evaporated milk can is very small.

The number of milk cans in a boxcar would be a good arithmetic problem, much better than the ones asking about what time trains would meet when traveling from opposite directions. I never got those right. I could have suggested that problem to the class, but Miss Rhodes wanted our class to start brainstorming about how to raise money to buy evaporated milk.

Miss Rhodes had blond hair and her blue eyes could switch from happy to sad or mad in a split second, but mostly they stayed happy. We all liked her, but we didn't admit it. We felt sorry for her because our pretty, nice teacher didn't have a husband.

Once, Billy's mom said she felt bad about Miss Rhodes being an old maid. I asked Mrs. Parker at what age a woman became an old maid, and she said age didn't matter, available men mattered, and they were in short supply. Mrs. Parker told me Miss Rhodes graduated from high school two years before my brother Johnny, so I figured out that Miss Rhodes was 26 or 27, pretty old. She'd probably never get married.

"I'll get us started." Miss Rhodes picked up a piece of chalk. "One boy made money for the Friendship Train by selling the shirt off his back. He sold the shirt, then the buyer gave it back, and the boy sold his shirt again." She wrote "selling shirt" on the blackboard and asked for other suggestions.

Virginia suggested a cake walk. Harvey said he could do yard work. Margaret came up with window washing. One of the chubby girls thought we should make candy. The chalk scratching put me in a trance, and I started thinking about how Mama and Johnny might feel about this train project.

Mama floated in and out of my thoughts these days and she didn't blame me for not fixing the hole. I could almost smell her rose perfume and picture her flipping pancakes, folding towels, mopping floors, singing with the radio, and smiling at me. I felt her fingers on my cheek when she'd kissed them and put them there the night before she died.

I never thought about Johnny being a soldier and shooting people. I remembered him teaching me how to hold a baseball bat, playing catch with me, and laughing. Johnny loved to laugh. He actually did look like Jimmy Stewart. If I turned out looking like Johnny instead of Papa, it might be okay. I wouldn't mind that.

"Jimmy, do you have anything to add?" The old maid's eyes twinkled. She knew I hadn't been paying attention.

"No ma'am."

"We're looking for ways to connect with French or Italian people," Miss Rhodes prompted.

Students whispered and giggled. I squirmed and felt my face get burning hot. Miss Rhodes waited, so I blurted out the last thing, the very last thing, I wanted to say.

"A family named Deschamps near Isigny, France helped my brother Johnny."

The twittering stopped because everyone knew Johnny got killed in the war. Miss Rhodes rested her hand on my shoulder a second, and then tapped her fingers in a miniature pat before moving to her desk.

"I think Jimmy's discovered what Drew Pearson is trying to promote, a personal connection with other people. Those people helped your brother, and maybe we can help them or people like them by sending food. Our class is to collect the money our school raises. Jimmy, I think you should be our treasurer."

Miss Rhodes named Margaret Allen and Virginia Mendez as reporters for the school projects. We'd have news galore since those two girls tried to outdo each other to be teacher's pet. Billy would collect press clippings about the Friendship Train, a swell task for him because his dad worked for the newspaper. Danny Metz and Dorothy Gallagher volunteered to collect the money from the lower grades each day, and turn the money in to the school treasurer — me.

Whoops! Everyone trusted Dorothy, but I had my doubts about Danny. Danny Metz is a kid who's always ready to fight. He took on anyone brave enough to rib him about his red hair, his crooked teeth, the big brown mole on his right cheek, or the hand-me-down clothes he wore. Plus, I knew for a fact that Danny hadn't always been honest.

On our walk home, I asked Billy what he thought about Danny being responsible for collecting money. As school treasurer, I was concerned.

"I don't know. I think he cheated off my geography test last week. He's no good at geography," Billy said.

"Yeah, well he wouldn't cheat off our spelling papers." I joked.

"Not if he's got half a brain." Billy laughed.

"Were you at the game when Danny refereed and he said the catcher tagged me out at home? I slid in safe, and Danny knew it, but he called me out. I'm still mad about that."

"Wasn't there, but you've told that story a million times." Billy shook his head.

"Well," I said, "the call makes me wonder about his honesty, you know." I turned my jacket collar up to keep the drizzling rain off my back. "You should tell the truth about baseball."

Billy nodded his agreement. "Hey, your Louisville Slugger's still in Mulkey's window."

"Guess it'll have to stay there. I'm giving my egg money to the train."

"I thought you were getting that bat for your birthday."

"Me too, but sometimes you get clothes instead." I shrugged and pretended not to care. "Hey, is Principal Collins married?"

"What?" Billy stopped walking and stared at me.

"Well, if he's not, maybe he could marry Miss Rhodes so she wouldn't be an old maid."

Billy looked at me like I'd lost my marbles.

"Forget it," I said and took the fork leading to my empty house.

"Yeah, I will. By the way, don't take any wooden nickels." The regularity of Billy's advice comforted me.

FIVE

Miss Rhodes let Danny, Dorothy and me eat lunch in our classroom and count money, which was great until Dorothy got out her stinky tuna sandwich. Miss Rhodes opened the window to let in some fresh air and some rain. Getting daily class donations to match the entire school amount reminded me of a teeter-totter. I liked seeing the totals balance.

"You're good at this, Jimmy," Miss Rhodes said. "Maybe you could be an accountant."

"I plan to play baseball for the Yankees."

Danny smirked and mumbled something to Dorothy who snickered.

"Well, maybe an accounting career could be a back-up plan." Miss Rhodes patted me on the shoulder.

After Mama died, Miss Rhodes had started touching my shoulder when she walked by my desk. I liked it, but I sure hoped the other kids didn't notice. They might accuse me of trying to be a teacher's pet like Margaret or Virginia.

The adults finally solved the math ratio problem about filling a boxcar with evaporated milk cans, and Principal Collins announced the cost would be about $8,000. Since you could buy a house for the same amount, the chances our school could fill an entire boxcar seemed unlikely.

Halloween fell on Friday, and Principal Collins suggested we trick-or-treat for pennies for the milk fund. Billy and I liked that idea and we dirtied our faces and carried hobo bags with us. Even though we were eighth graders, most people gave us treats and pennies for the fund. We counted the money at Billy's house, ate a couple of popcorn balls and all our good candy.

Saturday morning, my stomach didn't feel like coffee or food, so I made toast to go with my milk. I'd gotten used to making my breakfast, but not to the silence. Even after Mama quit cooking much, she'd always turned on the radio which provided background for our mornings. I tried tuning in her favorite programs, but their sounds made me sad. A knock interrupted my breakfast.

"Telegram delivery," a voice said when Papa opened the door.

Telegrams usually meant something bad, so I went to the living room to face the news with Papa. He opened the envelope and whistled. Papa wore a weird half-grin on his face, shook his head like he couldn't believe his eyes, and mumbled "Ida, Ida, Ida."

"What's wrong, Papa?"

"Nothing. We've received a message from the famous Drew Pearson."

"Yeah?"

"Listen to this." Papa held the telegram for me to see while he read it aloud. "LETTER RECEIVED STOP YOU AND SON ON INTERVIEW LIST FOR FT AMBASSADORS STOP CAN MEET YOUR HOUSE 7PM NOV3 STOP PLEASE CONFIRM STOP DREW PEARSON"

"Wow! That's in three days. Is Drew Pearson really coming to our house? What's an interview list? Why does it say you and son? What's an FT ambassador?" My questions bounced around like those Mexican jumping beans I'd seen at the carnival.

Papa sank into his favorite chair, and I perched on its arm.

"Pearson's been talking about putting an average person on the Friendship Train," Papa said. "Big shots, like state governors, city mayors, and movie stars will be aboard, but Drew Pearson wants someone to represent the ordinary Americans."

"We're ordinary," I said.

"I wrote Mr. Pearson about your mama and the money, and I offered to go as a railroad man, but I said I couldn't go without you. I never dreamed he'd even read the letter."

"Mama said you'd get to go, and now I'll be going too." I jumped up. "Wait till I tell the kids." I pictured Billy's excitement and Margaret's shock.

"Let's keep this to ourselves. The interview list could be an arm long."

"Can't I tell a few friends?" I mentally tried to cut the list of people I wanted to tell.

"Better not. We don't want Mr. Pearson mobbed by every Tom, Dick and Harry in Oakland." He made a line in the dust on the coffee table and raised his eyebrows. "We'll ask Martha to give us a hand cleaning and maybe she'd make her coconut cake."

"I'm taking our laundry to Martha today," I said. "I'll ask her. She's not going to believe Drew Pearson is coming to our house."

Papa told me to swear Martha to secrecy, and he went to telegraph Drew Pearson. I took my sheets off and added them and my Sunday pants and white shirt to the laundry. I heaved the bag over my shoulder and headed to Martha's, a big grin on my face.

This perfect day called for harmonica music. I played *Yankee Doodle* and had almost finished *Pop Goes the Weasel* when I passed Mulkey's Sporting Goods, and the day stopped being perfect. My bat had disappeared.

"The Louisville Slugger, did it sell?" I asked, pushing the door open.

"Sure did. Fellow about your age, red hair, long face, mole on his cheek. Know him?" Jerry Mulkey, the owner's nephew, acted proud of selling my bat.

"Maybe," I said. The description fit Danny Metz like a well-worn glove.

"Must have been saving a long time, 'cause he had mostly pennies." Jerry leaned on the counter like he wanted to talk.

I felt like I'd been punched in the stomach.

"You know the story behind the Louisville Slugger?" Jerry asked.

"Huh?"

Jerry played shortstop on the high school team and loved baseball like I did. "This woodworking shop in Louisville in the 1880s made bowling pins, columns for porches, and stuff." Jerry checked to see if I'd been listening.

"Yeah, bowling pins," I mumbled.

"Well, the owner's son worked in the shop, and he loved baseball, kinda like us. One day he went to a game and the best player broke his bat."

"And?" I only half-listened. I was picturing Danny Metz swinging my bat.

"The young man made a bat for the ballplayer who got three hits with it the next day. When the son took over, he changed the company into a bat-making business." Jerry grinned.

"I hoped I'd get the bat for Christmas."

Jerry saw my frustration. "Hey get rid of the long face. We'll get more before Christmas. Be patient."

I'm not a patient person, and I didn't play my harmonica after I left Mulkey's. I expected visiting Martha and the twins to cheer me up, but her place smelled like Vick's salve and no good aromas came from her kitchen. The twins sniffled with runny noses

46

and took turns coughing, whining, and begging Martha to hold them.

I told Martha about Drew Pearson's visit on Monday, and how Papa wanted to know if she'd make her coconut cake and tidy our house. I thought my news would cheer her up, but she didn't seem interested and didn't even ask me to eat lunch with them. I gave her the laundry bag and left her with two crying boys.

My bad weekend carried over to Monday when Miss Rhodes told me to go to the principal's office. I took my time putting my books away and trying to figure out why he wanted to see me. When anyone got sent to the principal's office, it didn't usually involve a pat on the back — the pat often landed lower.

"Ah, Jimmy Burns, close the door, please." Principal Collins sat in an immense comfortable chair behind his oak desk.

I knew closing the door meant trouble because I'd seen the letters, WALTER COLLINS, PRINCIPAL backwards on frosted glass before. I sat in a straight-back metal chair with little padding under the green leather. The chairs were very uncomfortable.

"I suppose you know why we're meeting." Principal Collins peered at me from behind his black-rimmed glasses.

"No sir."

Principal Collins leaned back, put his opposing fingers together and pushed them in and out, in and out—finger push-ups. I watched his exercise routine and he watched me.

"You're the treasurer for the Friendship Train money, aren't you?"

"I am." I spoke only when spoken to in this office.

"What are the treasurer's duties?"

"Well, Dorothy Gallagher and Danny Metz count money from each of the teachers, write it down, and give them back the envelopes for the next day. Then they give me all the money. I count it, and my total matches their sum of the individual classes." I didn't like this conversation.

"Sounds like a system that should work."

"It does."

"Actually Jimmy, your school total came up short by $1.82 on Friday. Now that money would have bought several cans of evaporated milk for those hungry boys and girls in Europe." He waited, then stood. "You can go now. I'd like you to search your conscience and come see me after lunch."

I stopped in the bathroom before I went back to class and kicked the tile wall next to the urinal. *Search my conscience! No sir, someone should search Danny Metz's conscience and his closet too. I bet he stole the Friendship Train money to buy my bat.* I pounded the wall 'cause I needed to hit something and Danny Metz wasn't around.

Since I couldn't hang out in a stinky toilet all day, I plastered a smile on my face and went to our room where the desks were arranged in groups. Miss Rhodes told me to work on a letter to a French or Italian student. I took my seat with Billy, Margaret, and Virginia, but instead of some French kid, I wrote to Billy. Margaret sat on my right, and she read what I wrote.

After I passed my note to Billy, Margaret slid me a folded paper. I didn't need her butting into my business, but I opened it anyway.

"Jimmy," her note said, "you are mean, but you are honest. Can you get the Friday records and see if the $1.82 matches any class contribution?"

"You think I'm mean?" I whispered.

"You're always mean to me," Margaret said, keeping her teeth together and trying not to move her lips.

I raised my hand and asked Miss Rhodes for Friday's money report. Margaret spied the amount before I did. The missing money matched the contribution from Miss Stone's class.

"That's my sister's class. She took in nine pennies last Friday, and she colored them red, white or blue," Margaret said, opening her mouth only on the left side.

I whispered, using the right side of my mouth. "Danny picks up from Miss Stone. What's wrong with your sister? Why does she color pennies?"

Billy kicked me and held both hands palms up. He wanted me to tell him what Margaret had said. Margaret elbowed me and passed a note saying her sister colored the pennies for our flag's colors, and we should make sure colored pennies were included in Friday's money.

"I didn't see any colored pennies in the money Dorothy and Danny gave me," I whispered. "I would have remembered. I think Danny stole the money and used it to buy a Louisville Slugger."

Margaret's next note had Louisville Slugger and four question marks.

I rolled my eyes. She really did not know, and I thought she had a great brain.

"It's a baseball bat, and Danny bought one from Jerry Mulkey on Saturday. Ouch!" I yelled out when Billy kicked me harder than he intended.

"I'd like to see you in the hall, Jimmy." My teacher's eyes did not look friendly.

"May I come too?" Margaret asked.

What a stupid question from old Margaret. Who asks to go to the hall with a teacher? Miss Rhodes led both of us out of the room. When we passed Danny's group, I heard him say something about Margaret and Jimmy in a tree, k-i-s-s-i-n-g. Miss Rhodes ignored Danny's comment, but I wouldn't.

Margaret spoke before the door whooshed closed. "Miss Rhodes, we've figured out what happened to the missing money."

Miss Rhodes looked at me, but Margaret talked. She explained about the missing amount matching her sister's class, about nine colored pennies, about Danny buying a Louisville Slugger from Jerry Mulkey, and she suggested we examine the pennies at school and at

Mulkey's Sporting Goods. She finished by stating the colored pennies would prove me innocent and Danny Metz guilty.

Miss Rhodes answered Margaret's speech by marching us to the principal's office where Margaret repeated the story while I sat in the uncomfortable chair and twirled my cowlick. I should have done the talking, but Margaret's never been in trouble her whole life, and teachers believed anything she said. Her magic worked on our principal too.

Mr. Collins unlocked the file box and retrieved the daily collections. Not one colored penny appeared in Friday's envelope. Mr. Collins confirmed with Miss Stone that the colored pennies had been given to Danny on Friday, and then he dialed the phone.

"Mr. Mulkey, this is Walter Collins from the school. I have a strange request. Would you check your till and see if you have any colored pennies in the drawer?" He paused. "That's right, red or white or blue." He listened, and then continued. "Swell. Would you put them aside? I'll stop by after school and explain, and I may bring a student with me."

When we got back to our room, Miss Rhodes told Danny to go see Mr. Collins, and his eyes looked so scared that I decided I wouldn't fight him about the k-i-s-s-i-n-g thing.

My day had been so full, I'd forgotten about Drew Pearson's visit. Today, Margaret spoke for me. Papa would have to do all the talking if Mr. Pearson chose us, but what if something happened to Papa? If I couldn't even explain something to my teacher, how could I possibly speak for the kids of the United States?

SIX

I peeked from behind our living room drape at the shiny black Packard gliding to a stop at 6:55 p.m. I knew the precise time because I'd been checking the clock ever since Martha brought her coconut cake and our laundry with my Sunday clothes.

Papa sat in his chair pretending to read the paper. He hadn't turned a page in the past seven minutes, so I thought Papa might have knots in his stomach, too.

"He's here," I said, "and I'm going to the bathroom before he comes in."

"That'll be your fifth time in the past hour." Papa folded his paper.

"I know, but I gotta go." I raced to the bathroom.

Maybe I had a disease. I wondered what sickness made you go five times in an hour. I hoped Papa wouldn't tell Mr. Pearson about me needing to go so often. If I had some strange illness, Papa and I might not get chosen to be Friendship Train ambassadors. After I finished, I hurriedly zipped my pants and then casually strolled into the living room.

And there he was. Mr. Pearson wore a double-breasted suit, and he stood a head taller than Papa, but his shoulders were rounded where Papa's were square. Mr. Pearson had a long nose, and his thinning light brown hair matched the sparse mustache. His beard stubble showed, and dark circles around his eyes made him look tired, yet he filled our living room with energy.

"You must be Jimmy." Mr. Pearson extended his hand and sized me up in an instant with his gray-blue eyes.

"Nice to meet you." I took his hand and looked him straight in the eye.

He smiled, which crinkled the lines around his twinkling eyes into furrows. In an instant, I knew Mr. Pearson would be able to look at someone and tell whether he was telling the truth or making up a whopper. My stomach flip-flopped and I felt a bit uneasy, even though I am not a liar.

"Mr. Burns, Jimmy, please accept my sympathy on the recent death of Mrs. Burns," Mr. Pearson said.

Papa murmured thanks, and I bobbed my head. People talking about Mama's death startled me because I still half-expected to see her scrambling eggs in the mornings or ironing and mending clothes in the evening. When he mentioned Mama, I glanced toward the dark kitchen, looking for her.

"Your telegram said my boy and I were in the running to be on the Friendship Train." Papa sat on the sofa and I slid in next to him.

"We received hundreds of letters, and checked the better candidates," Mr. Pearson said. "I wanted to meet the finalists in person. You can tell a lot about a man by shaking his hand."

"Not a lot to tell about me, Mr. Pearson. I'm a family man, a railroad man, a God-fearing man."

Uh oh, I thought. *Papa's ruining our chances. Maybe I should tell Mr. Pearson about Papa's safety awards or that he's a good father. I knew for a fact not all kids had good fathers.* I stayed silent, convinced Papa had spoiled any possibility we had to go on the Friendship Train.

Mr. Pearson leaned toward Papa. The voice I'd heard so many Sunday nights on the radio spilled from the man sitting in the chair we reserved for company. Questions and answers flew back and forth like the ocean coming in and going out. Mr. Pearson's words were sharp and pointed, Papa's rounded and easy. The men seemed to have forgotten me.

Mr. Pearson asked question after question: "Can you tell about your son's rescue by the Deschamps family after his parachute drop behind enemy lines? His death in combat? Your wife's fervent desire to do something for people like the Deschamps family? Where your wife's monetary gift came from? Why you wanted to ride this train?"

Papa fielded each question in a relaxed manner, and when the clock chimed 7:30, they were smiling and chatting like old friends.

"My Ida wanted me to do this, being on your train would honor her."

I thought Papa's comment sealed the deal. But then Mr. Pearson turned to me.

"Jimmy, your father will represent the adults who have seen the horrors of war, suffered through the depression, and who know about hunger. You represent the youth, a new generation willing to share its food with the less fortunate." Mr. Pearson's eyes searched my soul.

"Okay," I said lamely.

"I understand you're the school treasurer of the milk fund. Can you give examples of how students are raising money and why they want to give?"

I sat there with my teeth in my mouth. How did he know our school was collecting for evaporated milk? That I was the treasurer? Did he know about the missing money? About Margaret saving my reputation? The silence grew, blanketing the whole room.

I finally remembered something. "Well, uh, one little first grader colored her pennies red, white, and blue to honor our flag. Of course she didn't know we'd be changing those pennies for a can of milk."

"That's a swell story. Letters from young people and adults wanting to help the war victims in Europe fill my mailbag each day. Most are serious, but I get funny ones too."

"Tell us a funny one," I suggested. Maybe my brain could come up with another answer while he talked.

"Well, when I mentioned in one column about rats eating the grain we could use for flour, I got a letter from a man in Ardmore, Oklahoma, who said my column inspired him to kill 300 rats. He promised he'd kill more rats so the extra wheat could go to the families in France and Italy."

"How'd he kill them?"

Mr. Pearson laughed. "You know, Jimmy, my readers asked the same question, and the man offered to give his secret to rat-killing to anyone who sent him a self-addressed envelope. You want his address?"

"No sir! We don't have rats. I just wondered." I didn't want him thinking we had rats. We'd caught a mouse or two, but never rats.

"The committee has received donations from men in prison, from war widows, and from the very rich. The idea spread quickly. I first mentioned the food collection on October 11, and the train will begin its journey on November 7."

"I'm donating my egg money." I blurted out, finally remembering something I could say. "Kids are selling their crayons, babysitting or giving their lunch money." I babbled on, telling him about the food plate Principal Collins showed, the class projects, and the maps and letters we were adding to the milk cases.

Papa touched my arm to stop me from running off at the mouth. I don't know what got into me, 'cause I'm not a talker, especially to adults. I guess I wanted Mr. Pearson to like me.

Papa smiled at me and Mr. Pearson. "You can see that we're both enthusiastic about this train."

"Not everyone is." Mr. Pearson looked at Papa and then at me. "I must tell you that serious threats have been made. So serious, that your lives could be in danger."

"Why would anyone be against helping people?" I asked.

"There are two groups, the isolationists and the Communists." Mr. Pearson told me. "The isolationists think we did our part in the war, and they want us to focus on our country and our citizens. That sentiment seems strongest in the Midwest."

"And the Communists?" Papa asked.

"They'd like to take over the world, and they've made a good start." Mr. Pearson leaned forward. "Mr. Burns, Jimmy, the attack risk is real. You should consider that before agreeing to serve on the train."

"I thank you for your honesty, but I'm willing to go if you want me," Papa said.

"I'm not afraid, either," I said boldly.

Papa rubbed my head. "You know, all this talking has made me hungry. How about some cake and coffee, Mr. Pearson? My daughter brought her fresh-coconut cake, and I think it's the world's best."

"Then I must try a slice, but I'm a milk drinker, not a coffee drinker."

Mr. Pearson followed Papa into the kitchen, and I tagged behind them. As I got the good plates and cloth napkins, I noticed Mr. Pearson's eyes flitting around the kitchen like they were taking pictures. I bet he could have written a book about us after being here for an hour. I'd like to see his house. He probably lived in a mansion.

"Um, um." Mr. Pearson issued a contented sigh after tasting Martha's cake. "Tell your daughter this is definitely the best fresh-coconut cake I've ever eaten."

The journalist wasted no time finishing the big piece Papa had sliced for him. He leaned back in the kitchen chair and patted his stomach. Papa offered him more cake or milk, but he said no to both. I reached for the cake plate, because my piece seemed smaller than the men's slices, but Papa gave his head a half-shake, and I pulled my hand back.

"Robert," the well-fed Mr. Pearson said, "can you and Jimmy join the Friendship Train in Oakland on November 8?"

"You mean it?" I jumped from my chair, then quickly sat down and rested my chin on my fist. I wished I had stayed in my chair, but I hadn't.

Mr. Pearson talked to Papa and me like we were equals. "My secretary, Marian Canty, talked to Jimmy's principal. Mr. Collins asked that Jimmy keep a journal and write a daily article for the *Oakland Tribune.* Jimmy will also have a camera so he can document the Friendship Train journey."

I nodded several times, but clamped my lips together to prevent something stupid shooting from my mouth like the fact I'd only taken two or three pictures in my whole entire life.

"Good thing the bat situation got straightened out, Jimmy." Mr. Pearson winked at me.

I'd forgotten to tell Papa about Danny, the Louisville Slugger, and the missing money. I knew Papa would remember Mr. Pearson's comment and quiz me before bed.

"I've got vacation coming," Papa said. "You said the train would be in New York on November 18th, so I'd be gone less that two weeks."

"The head man at the Southern Pacific Railroad said not to worry about taking vacation time to help out. You'll work with the regular crew, Jimmy will help me, and everyone on the train helps with last-minute boxcar loading."

"You can count on me and my boy." Papa put his hand on my shoulder.

"Gentlemen, welcome aboard the Friendship Train." Mr. Pearson shook Papa's hand and mine, like I was a grown-up.

I listened to the car's engine start and stood in the open doorway to watch the taillights disappear. *Wow. I knew Drew Pearson, and he knew me.*

"Close the door, Jimmy. We're not heating the whole outside."

"I can't believe Mr. Pearson chose us. Can you, Papa?" I shut the door.

"I can't. We're going to have a busy five days. Could you get me a tablet from the junk drawer so I can start a list?"

"Sure, but first I've got to go to the bathroom."

For some reason, my urgent need to pee struck Papa's funny bone. Papa's laughter sounded good. He hadn't laughed in a long time.

SEVEN

Because Billy's dad worked for the *Oakland Tribune*, Billy treated our class to the latest stories from all over the United States. Billy gave good reports, but sometimes his voice squeaked at the wrong time and embarrassed him, so my pal felt nervous when Principal Collins asked him to speak to the whole school.

For the morning assembly, Billy wore a white shirt and a tie and he shifted his weight from one foot to the other while waiting his turn. I felt a little queasy myself, like I shared his anxiety. Billy looked a little green around the gills when he stepped to the microphone, so I gave him a thumbs-up sign when he looked my way.

"Hello." Billy started quietly. "The Friendship Train will be getting a real Hollywood send-off on Friday, November 7, with Eddie Cantor, master of ceremonies, and movie stars Glenn Ford, Ava Gardner, Elizabeth Taylor, and many others taking part."

The microphone screeched and Billy jumped back. Mr. Collins twisted the knob, tapped a couple of times, and said "testing, testing" before telling Billy to continue.

"The Friendship Train Committee is filming its journey across the United States to show in theaters in Europe. The firm crew . . . I mean film crew . . . wants train stations to be filled with ordinary people."

Billy's papers fell on the floor and everyone laughed except me. He scooped them up and struggled to put them in order.

"Students, remember your manners," Mr. Collins said sternly. "Billy, are you ready to continue?"

"I am. The movie will show that the food comes from everyday Americans and that neither the police nor military forced people to contribute." Billy sounded steadier. "So, if you're at the station on Saturday night, you could be a movie star!"

Students applauded which gave Billy confidence. "Oakland's parade will include scout troops, bands, Governor Earl Warren, and special Friendship Train ambassadors Jimmy Burns and his father Robert."

Billy mimicked a ringleader at the circus, pointed toward me and started clapping. A roar erupted, and I stood and waved like a politician, but I felt a bit sheepish. The last few days felt like a roller coaster ride. I'd experienced excitement and then terror because I'd never been out of California and I sure worried about meeting Mr. Pearson's expectations.

The teachers shushed the students after I sat down, and Mr. Collins closed with the surprising announcement that the eighth graders would be dismissed early on Friday. We'd help pack food, decorate boxcars, and construct parade floats. Our class cheered loudly until we got the evil eye from the principal.

Back in our room, Miss Rhodes handed us several purple-lined United States maps, still slightly wet with stinky mimeograph fluid. We'd had plenty of practice labeling states for the milk cases. Even kids who weren't good in geography whipped the maps out in record time.

Our teacher collected them and then asked if any students wanted to read their letters before she took them. Of course, Margaret and Virginia waved their arms and yelled "let me" and "I will, I will."

"Bonjour, je m'appelle Margaret Allen. J'habite à Oakland, en Californie. Je suis étudiante. J'ai deux soeurs. Je veux être votre ami." Margaret was too pleased with herself.

I nudged Billy and rolled my eyes. He put his hands around his throat and pretended to choke himself. Miss Rhodes eyed him warningly and asked him to read his letter.

"Well, I brought our class picture and printed 'Oakland eighth graders hope this milk keeps you healthy this winter.' I thought printing might be easier for them to read than my handwriting." Billy offered Miss Rhodes the picture.

Other students read theirs, and after I heard what they wrote, I stuffed mine in my spelling book. I'd brought a photograph of myself holding a baseball bat and had written on the back "Jimmy Burns loves baseball and the New York Yankees." What a dopey thing to do. What if I pulled a stupid stunt like that when Papa and I were on the train? Mr. Pearson would probably kick us off his train and we'd never get Mama's money to the Deschamps.

On Friday, the eighth graders went to the rail yard. Oakland would add seven cars on Saturday night. Two cars would have sugar donated by the Hawaiian territory. One would have flour from Vallejo, another would be filled with baby food from the Gerber Company, and the last three would be filled with evaporated milk, dried beans and peas, spaghetti, macaroni, and unscented soap bars.

Two older teachers manned the donation table. They turned down store-bought vegetables because of the water-weight, home-canned goods because the glass might break, and fruit because it would spoil. I hated seeing the disappointment on the people's faces when they got rejected. Their hurt reminded me of Mama's confusion over how to help the Deschamps family.

Students had their choice of jobs. The Friendship Train Committee provided an option of stickers written in French and Italian to place on all the food boxes.

The first said: All races, colors, and creeds make up the vast melting-pot of America, and in a democratic and Christian spirit of good will toward men, we, the American people have worked together to bring this food from our fields to your doorsteps, hoping that it will tide you over until your own fields are again rich and abundant with crops.

The second said: Just as we know that you, our neighbors, would extend aid to us in time of crisis, we the American people, make this offering of food and friendship to you when your need for food is as great as the whole world's need for friendship.

We all liked the second one better, but we alternated.

Our assembly line started with boys delivering milk cases to the girls, who inserted a labeled map and a personal note or picture. I noticed Virginia moved her lips in prayer each time she slid a map into the box. The next students glued the stickers, and the last group passed the milk cases to the railroad men and warehousemen who loaded the boxcars.

Danny Metz worked hard and kept his eyes down. I felt a tiny bit sorry for him because his mom and dad had loud screaming fights and the whole neighborhood heard. Danny also had to watch his brothers and sisters after school, and those kids were whiners and bellyachers, but he had stolen the money. Being an ambassador for the young people of America meant representing *all* kids, including Danny.

Other eighth graders painted French and Italian flags and the words "To our Friends in France and Italy from your friends in Oakland, California" on canvas. These banners were 30 inches tall and 12 feet long and every car needed a banner for each side. The high school boys made wooden frames for the banners so they wouldn't fly off when the train started moving.

Jerry Mulkey waved a hammer and motioned for me to come over. My back ached from lifting the evaporated milk cartons, so I rushed to see what he wanted.

"Your Louisville Slugger came back." He grinned.

"I know, but I used all my egg money for evaporated milk."

"Say, who's the stunner in the black plaid?" Jerry nodded to the sign makers.

I looked for a stunning beauty, but only Margaret Allen wore a black plaid dress.

"The one painting the French flag right now?"

"Yeah, she's gorgeous," Jerry said dreamily.

"That's Margaret Allen." I checked to see if we were looking at the same girl.

"I might give her a nickel and tell her to call me when she's sixteen."

"Margaret Allen?" I looked at Jerry and looked at Margaret.

"She's too young for me, but let me give you some advice. You better set your cap for her right now, because she's a head-turner."

"Margaret Allen?"

67

"Oh, yeah." Jerry stared at Margaret with a funny look in his eyes.

I didn't want to say "Margaret Allen?" again and sound like a broken record, so I punched Jerry lightly on the arm and told him I had to get back to work.

Gawking at Margaret, I tripped over a board. The high school boys hooted and pointed while I dusted off my pants. I sneaked a peek at Margaret to see if she had seen my fall. She had, but gave me an understanding smile. I never thought about Margaret being pretty, but Jerry knew about girls.

Later, I wrote instructions for Billy about taking care of my chickens. I'd miss them. I talked to my chickens about everything and sometimes they tilted their heads and looked straight at me with their shiny black eyes. When they did, I knew they wanted me to keep talking.

I'd told them my concerns about speaking to crowds, and being with adults I didn't know while Papa did railroad stuff. I told them my biggest worry — that the isolationists or Communists might attack the train like Mr. Pearson had warned. They'd probably force us to get off the cars in the middle of a snowstorm, and then we might freeze to death. The bad guys did that once in the Saturday morning cowboy movie, except the people didn't die because the hero appeared in the nick of time. My chickens listened to my fears, and I tossed them some extra grain.

When Billy showed up, he pretended to be confident about caring for my chickens, but he was nervous and the chickens could tell. They squawked, ruffled their feathers, and ran right at him. I hoped he'd learn to like them while I was gone.

"My dad's jealous that you're going to be with Drew Pearson for the trip. Mr. Pearson is his idol," Billy said as he scattered the chicken feed far from his feet.

"I'm supposed to send my stories to the *Oakland Tribune*. Mr. Collins said the paper would give me a byline. He acted impressed."

"A byline's just your name, tells the reader which smart person wrote the story."

"I'm not smart, not like big-brained Margaret Allen."

"You're smart enough." Billy kicked the dirt.

We both stood there after we'd closed the chicken coop, not saying anything. I kinda wanted to hug him good-bye, and I thought he felt the same way, but only babies, little kids, and old people hug.

I bumped his shoulder with mine and said, "Thanks for helping with my chickens. I'll see you in a couple of weeks."

Billy shook a warning finger and said in a deep gruff voice, "Don't take any wooden nickels."

We both laughed and he started up the path to his house. I watched him until Martha called me to come inside.

"The twins can't wait to see you and their grandpa in the parade." Martha folded my shirts.

"Papa and I get to ride in a convertible."

"Of course, you're big shots," Martha said. "We'll be on Seventh Street, so wave to the boys."

"Sure thing." I sat on the bed and watched Martha work.

"Do you know your stops?" Martha never paused in her folding and packing.

"You bet." I recited the list: "Sacramento, California; Reno, Nevada; Ogden, Utah; Green River, Rawlins, Laramie and Cheyenne, Wyoming,"

"Whoa! Write them down for me and leave the list on the kitchen table." Martha fastened the luggage and sat next to me. "You're a lucky fellow. You'll get to see America, 'from sea to shining sea,' like the song says."

Suddenly I couldn't breathe. I felt like I'd taken a punch in the breadbasket. "Martha, what if I can't handle the chores Mr. Pearson needs me to do? Almost any kid in our school—except Danny Metz—would be a better representative than me."

She put her hand on my cheek. "Jimmy, this is something new for you, and I think all people, kids and adults, worry about failing at something new."

"But what if I get tongue-tied and can't talk when it's my turn to make a speech?"

"If you fail, you'll make them feel good—they'll think they could have done a better job than the dopey kid on the platform car." Martha laughed and kissed my head.

My sister had spoken the truth. I hadn't seen many perfect kids in Oakland, so maybe all kids worried about getting picked for the baseball team, struggled with spelling tests, wondered why God did certain things, and sometimes cried secretly at night because a person they loved had died.

EIGHT

The band's bass drum boomed a heartbeat for the parade, which moved in measured paces toward the depot. Papa and I sat in the black convertible; well, Papa sat, but every time I recognized someone, I jumped up and shouted their name. This celebration felt like a party where everyone knew each other.

"Hey, Joshua, Caleb. It's me." I leaned their way and screamed to get their attention.

The twins sat calmly on their parents' shoulders until they saw us. Then they bounced around and tried to touch us. Little kids are so funny. They knew me and Papa would be in the parade, but they sure acted surprised when our convertible passed them.

The whistle shrilled and searchlights lit the sky as our part of the parade reached the station. The train engine decorations proclaimed "Friendship Train," and the next eight cars were painted red, white, and blue. The flat car with the searchlights also held loudspeakers shaped like a cheerleader's megaphone. A movie camera on a tripod panned the crowd, and I

72

remembered what Billy had said about us being movie stars.

Papa and I followed Governor Warren and his wife to the flat car for the ceremony. Mrs. Warren wore the biggest hat I'd ever seen in my whole life, making her easy to follow. After introductions, Governor Warren moved to the microphone.

"These gifts California is giving today will be like casting bread on the waters. Your generosity will result in deepening friendships between nations." His voice cracked with emotion two or three times.

If governors got nervous talking to crowds, I'd never make it. Then Mr. Pearson called my name. *Jeez Louise.* Governor Warren tugged on my left arm and Papa pushed my back. Then I was standing in front of a microphone looking at about a billion or maybe a trillion people, and they were all staring at me.

"Jimmy and I have something in common," Mr. Pearson started.

Good grief! What on earth is he talking about?

He continued, "My brother Leon and I kept chickens and went door to door to sell the eggs. You may have trouble believing this, but I was a shy youngster." Mr. Pearson paused for the audience's laughter. "When we went on our route, I knocked on the doors and then I stepped behind my little brother and let him talk."

"Oh, the eggs." The words flew from my mouth and echoed loudly from the speakers with a metallic sound.

"Jimmy, how did you get the money you donated to the Friendship Train?"

I didn't look at the crowd. I only looked at Mr. Pearson and answered his questions. I even told him I liked his egg story because now we knew even a famous radio broadcaster had once been nervous about talking.

"Maybe you'll be a broadcaster when you grow up," Mr. Pearson suggested.

"I think I'll be a professional baseball player."

The crowd cheered and whistled.

"Well, if your career doesn't work out . . ." Mr. Pearson started to speak.

"My teacher said if baseball didn't work out, I could be an accountant."

Mr. Pearson smiled. "Now you have another option. Thanks."

I could have chewed the fat even more, but Papa put his hand on my shoulder, a clue to keep quiet. I hadn't been afraid; in fact, I'd enjoyed speaking into the microphone.

Mr. Pearson told the crowd that Americans were giving food, time, and labor. He said some teamsters worked ninety-six hours straight in Los Angeles because they expected food for five boxcars but donations filled twelve. He praised the people for seeing and answering a need before the government got involved.

Then he introduced a French representative and an Italian representative. These two men spoke both in

English and in their own language. When they used their native language, they turned toward the movie camera.

A college glee club led the audience in *God Bless America* to conclude the program, and when we reached the mountains and prairie part, I spotted Billy. He wore an ear-to-ear smile. He'd probably been nervous for me just like I'd worried for him in the assembly, and we'd both done fine. We grinned at each other like a couple of baboons.

The festivities made me giddy with patriotism and happiness. The crowd didn't want to go home. Someone started *America* and then *Over There,* a song talking about the "Yanks" coming to help. The man aimed the movie camera at different spots, capturing the whole scene.

I pinched myself and didn't wake up in my bed. I'd performed the pinching ritual every day since Mr. Pearson's telegram arrived, and my left arm had a bruise to remind me this was really happening.

The famous radio broadcaster waved farewell and led us from the flat car into a club car. He started pounding the keys on a battered Corona typewriter, and only a woman holding two steno pads stepped inside the invisible circle surrounding him.

"Reno's mayor, Nevada's governor." Mr. Pearson spoke, but never stopped typing.

The woman made some scratchy marks on the first pad and turned to Papa and me. "I'm Marian Canty,

Mr. Pearson's secretary, and I have a camera, film and a writing tablet for Jimmy."

I dreaded admitting my picture-taking history involved pushing a button for someone else.

Mr. Pearson said, "Joe McCarthy's latest commie list before ten tomorrow morning. Can you believe McCarthy's suggesting all companies require loyalty oaths from their workers? That man is a menace."

Miss Canty scribbled again and said to me, "I have a camera like this. Would you like me to show you how to use it?"

I glanced at Papa to make sure he would listen too. Miss Canty showed me where to look, how to advance the film, and told me to record the picture number and information for each shot.

She handed me the camera and I took my first two pictures. I wrote: 1. Drew Pearson and 2. Marian Canty.

"Use the 5 *w's* and *h*—the who, what, when, where, why, and how for each picture. For example, your first entry should read Drew Pearson, typing news story, November 8, 10:30 p.m., after Oakland Rally, club car on Friendship Train."

"Marian, I need everything we have on the Marshall Plan. Jimmy, you need to include those *w's* and *h* in every newspaper article. You'll owe the *Oakland Tribune* a story tomorrow."

"Yes sir."

"Now, if you're comfortable with picture taking, we'll discuss letter chores." Marian pointed to a huge mail pouch next to her desk.

My brain hurt from having so many details sent to it, and I felt like a dumbfounded kid facing a professional pitcher's fastballs as Miss Canty's instructions on various topics whizzed by me.

"Open each letter, and then staple the envelope to the letter. Put them in five stacks and use initials "FT" for Friendship Train. You'll have: FT letters, comments on columns or broadcasts, FT contributions, praise or hate mail, and news tips. Sorting the mail will be a big help."

"George, could you get me a gin and tonic?" A man near Mr. Pearson's table held up his empty glass.

The columnist's head jerked up, and he stopped typing.

"Our porter's name is Samuel," Mr. Pearson said stiffly and then turned to me. "Some people call all porters 'George' for George Pullman, but we'll call all staff by their own names on this train. Jimmy, why don't you write your first story about Samuel?"

I agreed, because his question sounded more like an order than a question.

Samuel, dressed in a stiffly starched white jacket, returned with a drink for the man who'd called him George. He moved among the passengers refilling drinks, emptying ashtrays, and making notes for shoe shines and clothes to be pressed. His raisin-colored skin glowed with perspiration and his short curly hair

77

showed more gray than black. His eyes and actions anticipated requests, but his soft voice, unobtrusive movements, and permanent smile drew no attention.

Governors, mayors, and dignitaries went to a hotel for the night, but Papa and I stayed on board with the radio people, the camera men, reporters, and support crew. Samuel offered to show Papa and me our compartment, and we followed him to a sleeper car. I'd been on trains, but never spent the night.

"I'll convert the seats into upper and lower berths and draw the curtains when you're ready," Samuel said.

"Papa, I'll take the top one. Climbing will be easier for me, and more fun."

"The bathtub," Samuel said, "is located in the club car. I'll be happy to set an appointment for you. The men's lounge, where you may wish to change and shave, is at this car's end, right side, so you may hear people passing your compartment during the night."

"Can we go see it?"

"Hold your horses. Let the man finish." Papa placed his hands on my shoulders.

"Meals will be served in the dining car. We're using the best china and linens on this special train." Samuel said proudly.

I asked Samuel if he would answer some questions and he agreed.

"What is your full name?" I put the *w's* and *h* on the tablet edge to remind me the questions to ask.

"My name is Samuel Alvin Banks."

78

"Where do you live?" I scrawled his responses.

"I live in Chicago."

"How long have you worked?"

Samuel's smile broadened. "I've worked on the trains for twenty years. I start my day on the train at about five o'clock in the morning and finish about two o'clock the next morning."

"Then you only sleep three hours?"

Samuel nodded. "We are awake and ready before the first guest might need something, and you can't tend to other chores like shining shoes, pressing clothes, or restocking until all passenger needs are met. We porters catch up on our sleep between assignments."

I chewed on my pencil. "Do you like baseball?"

"Yes, my whole family loves the game."

We had something in common — we both liked baseball. "Who's your favorite team?"

"This year we cheered for the Brooklyn Dodgers."

"I'm a Yankee fan," I bragged. "We beat your team in the World Series, game seven."

"The Yankees are a great team. Our family cheered for Brooklyn because they put Jackie Robinson on the team. Young fellow endured a world of hurts, but he made us proud."

I never thought about things from Jackie Robinson's side, and didn't know what to say, so I changed back to Samuel's job.

"What work do you do each day?"

Samuel said, "All porters receive a book at least an inch thick listing do's and do not's. One rule is that porters always carry a tray. We joke about 'walking naked' if we don't have our tray with us. But the number one rule is 'smile.' In days before we had our union, I saw porters fired on the spot for not smiling."

I noted my answers and asked another *w* question. "What do you like most about your job?"

"I've traveled all over this beautiful country, met interesting people, even some famous ones, and I've saved my tips so my four daughters can go to college."

"Daughters? You're sending your girls to college. Why?"

"Well, Mr. Jimmy, working these routes I noticed the more successful people either have a special gift or a good education, so college for our girls became my dream."

I wrote his answer. Before tonight, I thought most girls wanted to get married and have a family, but this evening I'd met Miss Canty, who traveled across the country with her job, and Samuel who believed women should go to college. I remembered Margaret, the smartest person in our class, reading her letter in French and wondered if she had a big dream.

"Is there anything else?" Samuel asked with his ever-present smile.

"No. Thanks." I put my pencil in my pocket.

After Samuel left us, Papa and I realized our suitcases had been unpacked and our other shoes had been shined. I wondered when our porter managed to do those tasks.

"Jimmy," Papa spoke softly, "I've put your mama's savings in this money belt I'm wearing. I wanted you to know in case anything happened to me. Papa unlooped the normal-looking belt and showed me the money.

"You're okay, aren't you?" I didn't want him talking about something happening. Papa and Martha were all the family I had left.

"I'm fine, but you need to know these things. The belt money should go to the Deschamps family. I've got money for our whole trip in my billfold." Papa put the belt back on and buckled it. "Let's check out the men's lounge."

Fortunately, the ladies went to hotels at night, 'cause I didn't want to parade down the aisle in my pajamas in front of any women. Papa ruffled my hair and told me he wanted to visit with the other railroad men.

I got ready for my first night in the upper berth. I tried to sleep, but the evening's excitement and a quarrel I shouldn't have heard kept me awake.

NINE

Hey, Sleepyhead, rise and shine."

My body joins each new day in dribs and drabs. Sometimes my nose rouses first, like when Mama made biscuits or bacon for breakfast, or my eyes squint to keep out the bright light. Other times, my ears recognize the wind's howl, the rain's gentle patter, or my chickens' soft clucking. Being hot or cold makes me want to throw off the covers or burrow under the quilts, but what usually wakes me is the urgent need to run to the bathroom.

I sensed Papa's presence, and unusual sounds stirred in my brain. My eyes flew open and I sat up, banging my head on the ceiling. *Where was I?* Papa looked me straight in the eye, so this wasn't my bed. I rubbed the sore spot on my head.

"We're on the Friendship Train," I said.

"Yes, and you better get dressed unless you want to greet the people at Sacramento in your pajamas."

I didn't take long. I slipped the camera strap around my neck, put my harmonica in one pocket and my tablet and pencil in the other. In the dining car, Papa watched me hurry through some corn flakes and toast. When Samuel stopped to say good morning, I asked if Mr. Pearson and Miss Canty were working yet.

"Yes. Mr. Pearson works a long day," Samuel said. "He starts between five and six, works a couple of hours, has breakfast, and stays busy until late at night."

Oh brother. My first day to help Mr. Pearson and I'd be late. Papa and I headed for the club car so I could start my mailbag sorting, but a giant fellow in overalls blocked the corridor.

The man looked like a fighter. I'd never seen a boxing match — only posters promoting bouts, and an occasional fight scene in a movie — but this fellow seemed like a man who would run to trouble rather than away from it. His nose had taken a punch or two, and a pinkish scar zigzagged from his left cheekbone to the center of his square jaw. Huge muscles bulged under his blue work shirt, and I guessed most men would step aside for him. His flinty eyes lost no hardness when he offered Papa his oversized hand.

"I'm Thomas Pew," he said. "Hear you're back-up man on this run. Burns, right?"

"Call me Robert. Been railroading all my life, so I can handle most jobs. This is my boy Jimmy."

Mr. Pew tilted his shaved head toward me before continuing his conversation with Papa.

"The two of us will be coupling boxcars to the train. We can open the knuckles together, then I'll go to

83

the engine and you can signal." The big man turned sideways to let us pass.

"Thomas, I'll go with you now. Jimmy, keep your nose and your mouth clean." Papa touched underneath his bottom lip which meant I had breakfast left there.

In the club car, Miss Canty scribbled strange marks on her steno pad while Mr. Pearson talked nonstop. Being the only kid on a train filled with adults felt odd. I missed goofing around with my friends, but I acted grown-up and worked on my story about Samuel until a man wearing President Truman-style eyeglasses offered me his hand.

"Morning Jimmy, I'm George Welsh, President of the U.S. Conference of Mayors. I'll be on this train all the way to New York with you and your dad."

"How do you do." I'd done more hand-shaking in the past couple of days than in all the rest of my life.

"Our jobs are similar. You and your dad speak for the individuals, I represent the cities, and the governors are symbols for their states."

Some days I could talk a blue streak and other times my mouth seemed glued shut. Luckily, Mr. Welsh liked to talk and he didn't wait for an answer.

"Thought I might explain our routine so you'll know what to expect." Mr. Welsh looked at me.

I nodded enthusiastically. "Swell!" *Wrong.* "Uh, I mean, I'd appreciate knowing what's going to happen."

Mr. Welsh didn't seem to notice my mistake. "About twenty minutes before we arrive, the searchlights are lit and we start a short-wave broadcast. Once we stop, local people tell about their experiences gathering donations."

"Is that when we have to talk?" My stomach filled with butterflies again.

"No, Mr. Pearson speaks and he'll have the foreign representatives, Jean DuPard and Nicolo Guilii speak in their native languages. That's for the cameras. The film's being sent overseas so Europeans can hear about the train and America's generosity in their own tongue."

"I wondered why they talked in French and Italian."

"Newsreels are the reason, but immigrants fill our country. Many new war brides cry when they hear about the train in their language. Those brave women cross an ocean and start a new life, and most don't know our language."

I never thought about a woman's life until this trip. I'd only thought about women at home like Mama and Martha and then women without husbands like Miss Rhodes. Now, Miss Canty traveled across the country doing a job, Samuel wanted his girls to go to college, and Mr. Welsh spoke admiringly of war brides who couldn't speak English.

Mr. Welsh continued talking. "Mr. Pearson chooses different speakers from the train regulars at each stop."

My stomach dropped to the floor, and I grabbed a chair arm to steady myself.

"Nervous?" Mr. Welsh winked. "Just be yourself. Say something personal. I like to tell about my trip to Europe with other mayors when we took hand soap for token gifts. The people treasured those small bars. Our friends across the water need many things we take for granted."

His comment jogged my memory of the late night conversation I'd overheard. One man argued only Americans should have this food because too many soldiers died fighting over there. He said he planned to stop the train by hook or crook. The second man agreed that America shouldn't get involved in Europe's problems, but didn't want to do anything to hurt people. I bit my lower lip to help me think how to phrase my question.

"Everyone's for the train, right?" I prayed Mr. Welsh would say yes.

"Not everyone. Even Michigan, my state, has isolationists. They want us to put our heads in the sand, go back to the days before the world wars. They fear this food might go to the communists or to people we fought."

"Do you think people like that could be on this train?" I asked.

"Not likely, people on the train believe in its mission," Mr. Welsh said. "Mr. Pearson says giving Europeans food is like taking soup to a sick neighbor, and we're helping until they're better."

I twirled my cowlick and decided to keep my mouth shut. If the voices had been real and not a dream—and my dreams were so real I couldn't be sure—I couldn't identify the speakers. But why would anyone against the train be on the train?

"Do you have a warm coat?" Mr. Welsh asked.

His coat question caught me off guard. I'd been off in my own world, wondering if the men I'd heard were real. If they were, would they really try to sabotage the train? What did the "by hook or crook" comment mean? Mr. Welsh waited for an answer.

I stammered, "I, well, I brought the only winter coat I have."

"You'll need to bundle up tonight in Reno. The weathermen predict a temperature between 15 and 20 degrees when we get there."

"Brr. Thanks for the good information." I tapped my tablet with my pencil. "I'd better help Miss Canty."

Mr. Welsh gave me an approving slap on the back, and Miss Canty patted a chair and handed me a letter opener.

"You won't get many opened. We're getting close to our stop, but you'll have time to do the whole bag between Sacramento and Reno."

The first envelope I opened presented a problem—it had six dimes in it, and Miss Canty sensed my confusion.

"We put small amounts in a special fund for what we call the silver cars, food cars filled with donations of silver, the nickels, dimes and quarters we receive along the route or in the mail. Note the amount on the letter so we can write a thank-you to the giver and then put the money in this metal box."

Miss Canty gave a librarian's shush and inclined her head to the man who operated the short-wave radio. In no time at all, the engineer gave one long whistle, which Miss Canty said signaled the train was one mile from the Sacramento stop.

After the ceremonies, I glimpsed Papa and Mr. Pew on their way to couple cars. Their legs covered ground faster than mine, so I hustled to catch up. I photographed them individually and together as they opened the knuckles on the food cars, and I jotted down the "who, what, when, where, why, and how" like a regular newspaper man.

Mr. Pew went to the engine and Papa stayed by the food cars. Then Papa waved both arms in big circles straight out from his body. He looked like a huge bird struggling to fly. The engine backed slowly. The closer the engine came, the smaller the circles Papa made with his arms. Then Papa suddenly dropped his hands to his sides, and a loud crack confirmed the first Sacramento car's connection to the Friendship Train.

The Reno leg took a long time. We finished the mail, Miss Canty and Mr. Pearson typed letters, and I wrote my newspaper article. Mr. Pearson told me to put my story aside for an hour, then edit with fresh eyes before copying the final version on the Western Union Telegraph pad.

I knew Billy would save every story with my byline. Seeing my name in print would be swell. I might be as famous as a sports hero or a movie star when I went back to school. While I daydreamed about my future fame, I pulled out my harmonica and played softly, but soon people sang along with my tunes.

Mr. Welsh suggested *I've Been Working on the Railroad.* I played and they sang, and then someone suggested changing words so the song told about the Friendship Train. I must have started the song ten times. When we sounded really good, they quit singing and started doing grown-up stuff again. I wanted to keep playing, but the having fun faucet had been turned off.

Out of stuff to do, I weaved my way down the aisles to our compartment. I stared out the window at my moving geography lesson and compared what I saw to my U.S. map with the marked train route. I'd never seen mountains up close, and they stood so grand and glorious that their beauty sure made you believe in God. The wheels' music, the train's motion, and the dazzling scenery made me feel peaceful, a way I hadn't felt since Mama died.

After dinner, I finished my article, and it was so good I thought the editors might run my story on the front page. I gave the Western Union pages to Samuel and put on my coat for the Reno stop.

The freezing cold station bustled with activity. Papa spoke and I stood beside him. He did great! He didn't stammer, forget anything, or say "uh" over and over. One stooped lady with gray hair squeezed some coins into Papa's hand, saying her boy had been helped by the French people too. Her money would go toward a silver car. My heart felt full enough to bust.

Most train dignitaries went to the hotel for the night, but the Reno people had more loading to do. Even Nevada's governor, Vail Pittman, put food into the boxcars. Papa and I helped, but I got really cold, and when the lady who gave Papa the money suggested I run hot coffee to the workers, I could have jumped for joy.

I followed her to a tiny room in the station not much bigger than a closet, and the musty, dusty odor smelled like a closet. After an hour, the lady said she had to take her grandkids home and told me to leave the empty thermos jugs by the urn when I finished.

I warmed my red hands on the cafeteria-sized coffee urn while it percolated, then I filled and delivered the thermos jugs to the workers. I went back and forth until the coffee and my exhausted legs gave out.

When I returned with the last thermos, I unplugged the urn, turned off the light, and decided to take a short break before going outside in the below-freezing weather again. I rested against the wall, tired and content. My weary body slid toward the floor, and I moved my hands under my face for a pillow.

TEN

I shivered and pawed for my blanket and pillow and, not finding any covers, rolled over, pulled my knees to my chest, and tucked my freezing hands into my armpits. Cold settled into every pore. I struggled to lift my eyelids, but they seemed to have magnets attached and snapped closed each time I attempted to open them. I finally sat up. My bed was a hard, cold floor.

Jeez Louise. Where am I?

Only silence answered my question, but a light sliver led me to the door. The Reno depot, which had bustled with 4,000 chilly people, now stood curiously empty. I stumbled to a ticket booth where a thin-faced man studied numbers in long columns.

"Excuse me," I said.

His head jerked up, and he stared at me like he'd seen a ghost. His blue eyes turned mean. I must have interrupted some pretty important work, so I started to leave, but his voice stopped me.

"You're Jimmy Burns, aren't you?"

I nodded, wondering how he knew my name.

"Thought so. You match the description. Our men looked for you in last night's freezing weather. Churches held prayer vigils, and the Friendship Train delayed its departure an hour. Now you waltz in here, perfectly fine. Young people!" He shook a clenched fist toward me.

Did he say the train was gone? The tracks were empty. Had Papa gone with the train?

"Playing pranks in Reno is serious business, young man. I'm calling the police. Sit over there and don't move a muscle." He glared at me until I backed to the bench he'd indicated.

I piled up yesterday's newspapers, sat down, and didn't move a muscle. Questions raced through my head. What prank? Would the police put me in jail? How long? What did you do in a prison all day? What if my cellmate was a killer? Could I be a professional baseball player if I'd served time? Would Papa visit me? Where was Papa? How long had I slept?

My sound sleeping had botched things. The kids would laugh at me behind my back, if I ever got to go to school again. My stomach didn't feel so good. I swallowed to try and keep from embarrassing myself, but my tactic didn't work, so I grabbed some newspaper and heaved, covering the funny papers with last night's supper.

"What is wrong with you?" the man screamed. "Don't you have a lick of sense? You're going to clean your mess up, Mr. Troublemaker, and you'd better be quick about it."

I stared at the lake of vomit slowly soaking through the Sunday comics, afraid to move for fear the smelly mess would run down my pants. I eyed the closest trash can and duck walked toward my target, carefully balancing my offering.

"Can I go to the men's room?"

The man on the phone grunted and held up a towel for me. I'd cleaned myself up and scrubbed the bench and floor when the door opened.

Papa. I raced to him and squeezed his solid body until he pried my arms from around his waist.

"If he were my boy, he'd get a good licking," called the man from the ticket booth.

"Well, he's not your boy, he's my boy," Papa said. "I thank you for calling."

Papa called me his boy, but he didn't seem happy to see me, and he hadn't said a word to me, not a good omen. Papa never yelled, like some fathers did, but occasionally I wished he would, 'cause silence can be very loud. Papa cupped my elbow to guide me from the station instead of putting his hand on my shoulder—another bad sign.

"Alexander Woodall's offered us a ride to Ogden City, Utah. He drove Mayor David Romney over to Reno so the mayor could ride the train into Utah. If we're lucky, we can rejoin the train." Papa talked facts, nothing about me or last night.

"We might make it, Papa, because the train is splitting into two sections at Ogden City to cross the Rocky Mountains."

93

"We'll make it *if* we get there before the train leaves, and *if* Mr. Pearson wants us to continue after your disappearing act." Papa walked quickly. "Once we get on the road, we'll be having a long talk about your behavior."

I'd studied the train's route in detail, and I knew the four hundred mile distance from Reno to Ogden City would allow ample time for Papa's lengthy talk. Sometimes I thought kids got off easier with a licking than a talk, because a licking only hurt for a short time.

***

"Hey folks, I gassed up the Chevy, got us some sandwiches, and put your suitcases in the back. I'm ready when you are, Mr. Burns." The man speaking, Mr. Woodall, and my teacher Miss Rhodes looked about the same age. If the car driver wasn't married, maybe Miss Rhodes could move to Utah and marry him. Her old maid status bothered me.

Mr. Woodall's large head topped a tall, skinny body and his ears belonged on a much bigger person because they stuck out more than normal. You couldn't miss those flappers because his closely clipped hair magnified them. But when he smiled, you forgot about his big head and his big ears, because his grin talked, saying "I'm happy," and "I like you." I bet he never worried about anything.

94

I liked Mr. Woodall right off the bat and wanted him to like me. I regretted that he'd be hearing Papa's lecture. Still, the talk would be easier than jail time with a killer.

Papa watched for road signs and helped Mr. Woodall navigate until we left the Reno city limits. Then Papa leaned over the seat, and I knew my time had come. I sucked in a deep breath and straightened up. In my younger days, I tried to explain things, but after I got older, I learned to keep my trap shut until Papa asked me to talk.

"Jimmy, a man must be responsible for his actions, and last night you let a lot of people down. One man got frostbitten fingers looking for you. A nice lady going to a prayer meeting on your behalf slipped on an icy sidewalk."

I opened my mouth to ask if they were okay, but Papa wagged his pointer finger at me.

"They're both fine, and we should thank God they are, but the endings could have been different. Your thoughtless behavior put nice, helpful people in danger. Remember, a man's actions never stop with him."

Papa got quiet, but didn't turn around, so he hadn't finished.

"The other thing is between us. Jimmy, I need to know where you are at all times, because...well, because I do." He paused. "I've outlived two sons and my sweet Ida, and when you didn't show up last night, I felt like a big locomotive had flattened me."

95

Papa's shadow-rimmed eyes looked so weary I wanted to put my arms around him, pat his back and whisper "there, there" and "everything's going to be fine" until he felt better, but he sat in the front seat and I sat in the back.

"Oh Papa, I'll tell you everywhere I go for the rest of my life."

Papa shook his head side to side. "Why don't you keep me informed until you graduate from high school?"

"I'll do it, I promise." I leaned forward to put my hand on his shoulder. "And I'll ask God to bless all the people who looked for me last night."

Papa faced the front, and Mr. Woodall said we needed to stop for gas.

"Jimmy, why don't you get up front with me and let your father stretch out in the back seat?" Mr. Woodall didn't add that Papa not getting any sleep last night was my fault.

In no time at all, we heard soft regular snoring from behind us. Speaking in a low voice so he didn't wake Papa, Mr. Woodall told me stories about Ogden City and how his ancestors came to Utah to settle. We were sharing a sandwich when I saw a seagull.

"That gull must be lost; those birds stay near the ocean."

"Oh, we've got gulls in Utah, even a statue honoring them. They saved the pioneers. It's a sickening story. Want to hear it?" Mr. Woodall wrinkled his nose and made a face.

I couldn't wait.

"You asked for it." Mr. Woodall grinned. "The first settlers planted their crops, but when they got ready to harvest, swarming insects filled the skies. Some called them crickets, others locusts or grasshoppers, but everyone agreed their presence resembled the plague in the Bible, because those insects ate everything in sight."

"I like those plague stories in the Old Testament, but I'd hate to live through one. What happened?"

"Well, the people fasted and prayed and stomped on those insects, and even tried burning them. Nothing worked. Then the gulls came."

"How'd they help?"

"The birds ate the insects, drank water, and here's the sickening part," Mr. Woodall said cheerfully. "Those gulls puked up, or regurgitated those insects and came back for more. They stayed at it until the crops were saved."

"My friend Billy will love that story." I wrote gull story on my notepad so I wouldn't forget to tell him.

"Are you sure the bird vomit part won't bother him?"

"Nah. Billy's got a strong stomach."

I sure liked Mr. Woodall. He loved his hometown which sat between the Great Basin and the Wasatch Range. The basin lay flat as a bowling lane until the jagged Wasatch Mountains poked at the blue sky. Seeing America this way was better than looking at pictures in a geography book or making salt maps to feel the land's highs and lows.

I saw a sign for Promontory Summit, where they drove the Golden Spike connecting the railroad across the whole continent. I woke Papa, because he was a railroad man and I knew he'd want to see the spot.

"Hate to tell you, but that track section doesn't exist. They took the rails in '42 for use in the war." Mr. Woodall sounded apologetic.

I sighed with disappointment. I'd interrupted Papa's sleep for nothing.

"I'm glad you woke me. It's the history that matters." Papa rubbed the back of my head, and I felt everything was okay between us again.

"That's Ogden City, and the train's still there," Mr. Woodall said.

He pulled a big card from the glove compartment and told me to hold the sign against the windshield. The paper had the open sesame power, because the policemen ushered the car through the congested streets and straight to the station.

Mr. Woodall gave me his address and asked me to mail him my newspaper stories. We'd batted around ideas during our trip and I planned to include something about him in my next article. Before he left, I gave him a big hug. Hours earlier, I promised Papa I'd behave like a man and then I hugged Mr. Woodall like a two-year-old.

Mr. Pearson seemed happy to see us. Everybody called me some name, but Jimmy wasn't on the list.

They christened me Rip Van Winkle, Lost Sheep, Little Boy Blue, Sleeping Beauty, or Hibernating Cub. Each new name brought rousing laughter, except from me.

"Nice to have you back, Mr. Jimmy. We've missed you and your harmonica." Samuel used my real name and handed me a cola and a glass.

Being back on the Friendship Train felt terrific. The train lurched forward and we moved toward the mountains and the snow. I'd decided during the drive to Ogden City I'd find those men who wanted to sabotage the train and stop them, which was the least I could do for causing such a ruckus. When I exposed their evil plan, Papa and everyone would be proud of me and they'd forget all about my falling asleep in that closet.

ELEVEN

My mind churned with thoughts about how to crack *The Case of the Train Saboteurs*, a great book title I'd made up for my adventure. Since I already wrote for a big city newspaper, writing a mystery novel about the train should be no big deal, but getting a book published would be easier if I solved the case first.

All great detectives had sidekicks, and the first part of my plan involved getting a helper. Sherlock Holmes had Dr. Watson, Nero Wolfe had Archie, and the Hardy Boys had each other. Too bad Billy was in Oakland, because we could solve this case in nothing flat.

Papa couldn't be my assistant. I wanted to surprise him by solving the case on my own. Maybe Samuel or Mr. Pearson might help. Samuel rarely slept, so he might have already overheard important facts. Drew Pearson would be a great assistant, because he routinely solved cases and exposed government officials for wrongdoing, taking bribes, or stealing.

Papa said newspapers acted like watchdogs for us and that Mr. Pearson was a bulldog. Since catching bad guys would require bulldog determination, I decided on the journalist as the ideal sidekick. I hung around until Mr. Pearson took a break and then casually struck up a conversation.

"Mr. Pearson, my best friend's dad works for our newspaper, and he'd like to know how you find out about people who aren't doing what they should."

"I follow the loose thread and unravel the mystery."

"Really? I love the Hardy Boys!" I couldn't believe my luck. I'd wanted to bring up solving mysteries, and Mr. Pearson had done it for me.

"I use my eyes, ears, and nose to uncover a story." Mr. Pearson pointed to each body part for emphasis. "If something doesn't look, sound, or smell quite right, I ask questions."

"The reporter questions?" I was proud of myself for remembering.

"Exactly. If I see a representative's wife wearing a new diamond or mink, I might shock him with a phone call after he's asleep or arrange a face-to- face and surprise him with 'Did you buy your wife's beautiful mink with the money you got from a certain lobbyist?' Then I watch and listen."

"Doesn't he say no?"

"If he's honest, he'll be ready to punch you in the nose for questioning him, but if the man looks uneasy, stumbles on the reply, or if you get a whiff of fear, you know he's involved in something."

"Sounds simple."

"That's only the first step. My investigative team digs into every detail until we can prove or disprove the story. I've been sued for libel many times, but I've never lost a case."

"Libel?" I didn't know that word.

"Libel is a false story printed to hurt someone's reputation. Senator McCarthy makes accusations without checking facts, but he only calls specific names on the Senate floor where he can't be sued."

"Then all those people he says are commies might not be?" I was surprised.

"Right. McCarthy threatened me, told me he was going to name me as a possible Communist, so I mentioned to him that I had friends with the IRS." Mr. Pearson laughed. "He never followed through with his threat."

Miss Canty joined us, carrying a newspaper and her ever-ready steno pad.

"Look at Princess Elizabeth and her Lieutenant Philip. Doesn't she look radiant? I can't wait for their wedding." Miss Canty pointed to the news photo for us to admire.

"Marian's letting me know it's work time. Let me give you another tip, Jimmy. Women love romance, don't forget that."

"No sir, I won't." I knew Mr. Pearson wanted to get back to work, so I jumped in with my real question.

"Uh, you know, being on this train has been swell, but you and Mr. Welsh said some people opposed the train, so I wondered how someone might sabotage this train."

"Well, if an adult asked a comparable question, I'd be watching his every move." Mr. Pearson cocked his head to the left and stared at me with his soul-reading eyes.

"Oh, don't worry about me." I rushed to reassure him. "Billy and me like to pretend we're the Hardy Boys. I thought writing a mystery called *The Case of the Train Saboteurs* would make me rich and famous, but I'd share my mansion with Billy, and I'd let him drive my fancy cars."

Mr. Pearson smiled his approval, and I rushed on with my speech.

"Then I'd concentrate on baseball all the time and forget about being an accountant or a newspaper man, or a railroad worker. But to write my book, I need to know how someone might sabotage a train, and I don't have a clue." My lengthy speech used all my breath.

"Since this is an exercise, think about damage to the train itself, damage to the boxcar contents, or damage to the Friendship Train's spirit. *You* tell me tomorrow how someone could sabotage the train." Mr. Pearson winked and turned to begin work with Miss Canty.

That wink was a big relief, 'cause I can't always tell about grown-ups. I made three columns on my paper and wrote the words "train," "contents," and "spirit" at the top and waited for inspiration, but none came.

For phase two of my plan, I needed an alarm clock. I intended to sneak out at night and hear the plotters again. Of course, I'd leave Papa a note telling him I'd gone for a walk, which wouldn't be a lie, and I'd be back before he noticed I'd left my upper berth.

I caught Samuel leaving the club car.

"Samuel, I've been thinking I might need an alarm clock because, well you know about my sleeping problem in Reno. Do you know how much one would cost?"

"I'd be happy to give you mine for the trip. I always pack one, but never need it." Samuel led me to a small closet close to the chair where he slept. His seat was under a buzzer board, so he could be called even during his three-hour sleep time.

"Thanks for the clock. I'll never oversleep again."

"Anything else?" Samuel, tray in his left had, appeared eager to get back to the club car.

"Well, I do have a few more questions. I've been wondering if most men go to bed at the same time, or if certain ones stay up later than others."

"Oh, folks have their own rhythms, Mr. Jimmy. Some get up early, like Mr. Pearson, and others stay up late, like Mr. Pew, the railroad worker."

"Is he the only one who stays up late?"

"He and his friends share drinks and play cards. After Mr. Pew turns in, I finish my work. When we have young people traveling with us, they go to bed early and get up late, because they're growing."

"Samuel, what do men talk about when they're playing cards?"

"Oh, they joke about the cards, the good or bad hands, the train's progress, jobs to be done, or a pretty lady they saw at a stop." Samuel paused. "You know, Jimmy, I think your dad would be honored to answer your questions about becoming a man."

Good grief! My whole face got hot, even to the tops of my ears. I swallowed, shook my head, held up the clock in a voiceless thank you, and hightailed it to our compartment. I hoped Samuel wouldn't say anything to Papa.

Despite my awful red-faced moment, I'd learned Mr. Pew and his buddies stayed up late, and I had an alarm clock set to ring at midnight. I planned to sleep with my ear on the clock, confident I'd be able to push the off button before Papa heard the alarm.

The mountains wore a snowy dusting, and the falling flakes entertained me until time for dinner and the stop in Green River, Wyoming. Papa and I shared a spot on the program, and then I hurried to bed, thinking about my secret plans.

"You're turning in early," Papa said.

"Yeah, maybe if I get more rest, waking up will be easier."

"Good idea. I'm going to see what the guys are doing. Sleep tight."

I settled my head on the pillow covering the alarm clock and my note about my whereabouts for Papa.

When I got into my berth, Papa pulled up my covers and I felt guilty about my planned spying adventure.

The alarm rang at midnight, and I was fully awake, a miracle. Maybe I'd never gone to sleep. I peeked at the lower berth and saw Papa's empty bed. No spying for me tonight. I hid the clock and my note and slept until Papa jostled my shoulder the next morning.

Big smiles greeted me in the club car so I checked the zipper on my pants and wiped my mouth to make sure no eggs or toast crumbs lingered.

"We're going to sing the Friendship Train song at our stop in Cheyenne this afternoon. Have you got your harmonica?" Miss Canty asked.

"You bet!"

We practiced the song we'd made up to *I've been Working on the Railroad*. Albert Gaston, who usually helped with the radio broadcasts, told us where to stand and directed our singing.

The most noticeable thing about Mr. Gaston wasn't his appearance, but his extremely low-pitched voice, a surprise coming from a small man. He looked like Charlie Chaplin — without the mustache — because of his size, his jerky movements, and his constantly moving eyes.

Mr. Gaston asked Mr. Welsh and Mr. Guilii to stand in the center since they had the best voices. He assigned me to play and to yell a greeting or wave when they sang my name. We practiced our song with the new lyrics to the old tune.

The Friendship Train left California,
With food for France and Italy.
American people kept on giving,
What a show of generosity.
Can't you hear the commies crying?
'Cause no one believes their lies.
We'll be there to help our neighbors,
With food and medical supplies.

Pearson won't you wave?
Welsh, won't you wave?
Robert, won't you wave your hand?

DuPard, won't you wave?
Guilii, won't you wave?
Jimmy, won't you wave your hand?

Someone's filling cars in Chicago
Someone's filling cars, I know
Someone's stocking cars in Jersey
This train just grows and grows.

Fee, fie, fiddle-e-i-o,
Fee, fie, fiddle-e-i-o-o-o-o.
Fee, fie, fiddle-e-i-o.
To the New York harbor we go.

I would definitely include the lyrics in my next newspaper article. I bet songwriters made big money. Maybe I could play baseball and write songs, but I actually didn't write the words, so maybe I should forget that idea. When we sang, each named person said a quick hi or hey and waved their hand — except Mr. Pearson who never stopped working during our rehearsal.

After we finished practicing, Mr. Pearson signaled to me.

"Did you figure out the villains' methods for your train mystery?"

"Some," I said. "The bad guys could blow the train sky high with a bomb or wreck the cars by derailing them somehow. On the contents, I thought they might burn the bags and boxes, throw stinky stuff into the cars, or fill the cars with water. I decided water would be the best way to destroy the food."

"Why would dousing the contents be worse than burning them?"

"Burning might destroy the cars and I thought my bad guys would only ruin the food. Wouldn't water cause the flour, sugar, wheat, macaroni and spaghetti to swell up or rot?"

"True. For the cars with bulk shipments, the railroads have steamed the cars to kill weevils, but excess moisture can spoil the grain. Jimmy, what about the train's spirit?"

"That's harder. I'm not sure. Do you remember when the train passed through Rock Springs, Wyoming, and it was so snowy and windy you could barely see, yet people came out just to see the train?" I looked at the newspaper man.

"Yes. Train didn't even slow down, but the townspeople were there, indicating their support."

"That's how most people feel about the train," I said. "I guess a bad guy could say rich people, not hungry orphans would get the food, but he'd have to prove it, and he couldn't, could he?"

"I like your questions. We tried to anticipate problems like the ones you're asking. Our world just ended a horrible war where we proved we could destroy mankind. Now we need to demonstrate we can save it."

"I thought writing a good mystery might make me rich and famous, but I certainly don't want anything to happen to this train or to you, Mr. Pearson."

"Certain people in Washington wouldn't mind if something happened to me, but I think my readers and my listeners might miss me."

"Papa and I would. We listen to you every Sunday. You seem to talk a lot faster on the radio than in person."

"I do. Good observation. I have to give a whole week's news during my time, so I speak quickly. Jimmy, you're doing a swell job with your stories and speeches. You're a good ambassador for our young people."

I immediately wrote Billy telling him what Mr. Pearson said. I knew my pal would tell me I had the big head, but he'd be happy for me. I told him about the country I'd seen, the gull story, and the snow. I didn't mention my detective work, just in case his parents read my letter.

I went to bed early again, and when the alarm sounded at midnight, Papa snored contentedly. I tried to be invisible when I tiptoed down the aisle, my back against the wall, acting like the Hardy Boys did sometimes.

Murmuring voices stopped me before I reached the third car. Two men stood on the landing between the cars. I recognized both. The size and shape marked Thomas Pew, and the deep voice identified Albert Gaston. Our chorus director looked like a kid standing next to Mr. Pew.

"We need to do the job before Chicago when they split the train into two sections," Mr. Gaston said. "I've got friends in Illinois who'll help us get away."

"You sure you want to do this?" Mr. Pew asked.

"Absolutely. This food belongs in America. People will love us. Why is the government calling for us to cut back on our meals when this train is packed full of food? Why should we send our food to Europe? We already saved their hides in the war."

"I'm calling it a night." Mr. Pew flicked his toothpick into the passing dark.

I got a sudden chill, sidestepped hurriedly down the hall and climbed into my nice warm berth, but I couldn't sleep. A good journalist, or spy, needed to know the *w*'s and *h* of every story. I knew two, who was involved and why they wanted to destroy the train, but I needed to know when, where, what they planned to do, and how they planned to execute the plan in order to save the train.

TWELVE

At breakfast, Samuel told me we had crossed the state line into Nebraska about one in the morning. I checked our scheduled stops and my map. We'd be in Chicago on Friday. I only had two days to stop Mr. Pew and Mr. Gaston. Since the train would be divided in Chicago with half the cars taking the New York line and half the Pennsylvania line, I guessed they'd attack the train before the split.

Toting my camera, notepad, and a wad of courage, I headed toward the club car, planning to interview Mr. Gaston, villain. He wouldn't think my behavior strange since I'd been taking pictures and writing stories every day. My suspect snoozed in a chair, but when I clicked the camera button, he opened one bloodshot eye to see what had disturbed him.

"Sorry to bother you, Mr. Gaston. I realized I didn't get your picture directing our chorus yesterday, and I wanted to include you in my journalistic scrapbook." I thought my words sounded important and believable.

"Forget it. We won't be singing again. Mr. Pearson thought our performance changed the program mood. People are excited about the train, but reverent, and he felt our light-hearted ditty spoiled the ceremony. He's the man in charge, so it's out."

"I'm sure he knows best. Say, since I woke you, could I get my interview?" I wanted to get him talking before I lost my nerve.

"Get lost. I'm a boring fellow."

"Well, uh, now you've given me a challenge," I sputtered with more courage than I felt. "Mr. Pearson says every person has an interesting story. Why don't you start by telling me how you got on the train?" I acted all buddy-buddy and hoped the evil man didn't notice my shaky voice.

"I'm good with the radio, and this train has two radio operators—the man who does the Voice of America and the short-wave fellow. I'm back-up, like your Papa, and help out when needed."

"Did Mr. Pearson interview you? He came to our house."

"No. I talked to the radio men, offered to come on, and they agreed."

Mr. Gaston crossed his arms, let his chin fall toward his chest, and closed his eyes—but I needed to keep him talking.

"Were you at the Hollywood send-off?"

"Yeah. I live in Chicago, but was in California visiting my sister when this train deal started to get publicity. So, being a smart guy, I hooked on, and got free transportation home." Mr. Gaston sat up and sighed loudly, annoyed with my persistence.

"Home? New York's the finish. You can't miss the best part!"

"I won't miss the best part." He laughed. "But I am hopping off in Chicago. You won't go blabbing about my plans, will you?" My suspect raised his eyebrows and waited for my reply.

I dropped my pencil and crossed my fingers before I spoke so my lie wouldn't count. "I won't tell a soul."

"You ever been to Chicago, kid?"

"Never left California until now. Seeing our country is great."

"I never wanted to see the country. I was happy right where I grew up, a coal mining town in Knox Township, Illinois. Went into the mines after high school and worked my way up to blasting before my greeting from Uncle Sam arrived. Four buddies and I signed up to see the world, but all we saw were battlefields."

"My brother jumped from airplanes."

"I know. I've heard your speeches."

"Since you knew about blasting, did you get to blow things up in the war?" I hoped he'd spill his guts and allow me to close the case.

"Sometimes." Mr. Gaston actually smiled. "I guess all kids want to know about blowing things up."

"I don't know about other kids, but I sure do." I urged my feet to move a little closer, but they wouldn't move, so I leaned toward him.

114

"Ammonium nitrate," he whispered. "We used it in the coal mines and in the war. Stuff can cause an incredible blow. You remember the Texas City explosion this past April where 576 people died?"

"Yes." I kept my face calm even though my stomach cramped. I hoped he wouldn't tell me he'd killed all those people.

"Well, ammonium nitrate started the big explosion in Texas City. The blast force lifted a huge ship from the water, and you know what, ammonium nitrate is a fertilizer, easy to buy, easy as pie."

I gasped for air. I couldn't breathe. Could a 13-year-old kid have a heart attack? Papa would be really sad if I had a heart attack, considering how upset he'd been when I fell asleep in Reno.

Mr. Gaston stared at me and then slapped his knee like he'd heard a great joke.

"Look at your face. You're scared." Mr. Gaston poked the center of my forehead. "Rest easy, kid. The Texas City explosion was a big, bad accident. I didn't start the explosion, and to tell you the truth, I didn't get to blow up many things in the war either."

He motioned for me to get closer, put his lips close to my ear, and said, "BOOM."

I jumped about a foot. He laughed and ruffled my hair. I pulled back, because Papa tousled my hair when he wanted to set my mind at rest, and mean Mr. Gaston didn't have the right. I tapped my pencil on the notebook and acted professional.

"So, what did you do in the war?"

He stared at the Nebraska prairies racing past the windows before he answered. "My buddies and I asked to stay together, so we were what they called cannon fodder. Five went overseas, but I came back alone. We fought in the same places they're planning to send this food."

"Then you know how much they need the food, right?" I said softly.

"If you say so. In my opinion, we gave those people plenty. My friends, the guys who died, they have families. I don't see anyone knocking on *their* doors with food to feed *their* kids."

"But they're not starving, are they? My principal told us the kids overseas only get about one plate of food for a whole week."

"Right." He shook his head in disgust and snorted. "I bet you've swallowed more than one lie—hook, line, and sinker. You'll see the light when you grow up."

I snapped more pictures and smiled at him with my face, but not with my heart. I didn't like the detective business. I didn't want to believe people did mean things on purpose. Still, I felt a little sorry for Mr. Gaston who'd lost all his friends.

A real detective would have quizzed Mr. Gaston more about being a blaster, and a real detective would have found out how he'd blown things up. But if I'd asked him any more questions, he might have gotten suspicious. If he planned to blow up a train, rubbing out a kid would be a piece of cake.

I dashed to the toilet and made it, thank goodness. We kept matches in our bathroom for stinky times like this, but I didn't have any. After I finished, I hurried back to the club car and hoped nobody noticed I'd come from the john. I eased into the room, filled with noisy chatter, and pretended to be interested in Mr. Pearson's story. He sat behind his typewriter and looked like a king holding court.

"The Friendship Train idea started," Mr. Pearson said, "when I read several newspaper accounts about celebrations in France because the Soviets sent a shipload of free wheat to Marseille."

Mr. Welsh interrupted. "We've been sending free wheat on a regular basis, but without fanfare."

"We know the commies are trying to buy the minds of the Europeans when some dictator signs off on a load of wheat." Mr. Pearson checked his watch. "That's what started the wheels turning for me. I knew Americans had to show the Europeans that we were their real friends."

"I heard the inspiration came from your Quaker beliefs." said Mr. Guilii.

"That's true too. Aren't all our actions based on our beliefs?" Mr. Pearson challenged.

People in the car moved away from Mr. Pearson when he mentioned his faith. Some people are uncomfortable talking about religion, even me. Why, I've never asked Dorothy Gallagher why she eats fish on Friday, or why she calls all priests Father, and I really wanted to know. Maybe when I got back to Oakland, I'd ask her.

I moved closer to Mr. Pearson. "Sir, I'd like to hear about your Quaker beliefs."

"So, our budding reporter wants to know. Is your pencil sharp?"

I nodded and pulled out my tablet.

"I'll keep it simple," Mr. Pearson said. "In fact, simplicity is an important principle. Quakers believe God dwells in everyone and that people show their faith in four ways—simplicity, stewardship, peace, and education."

I wrote the four items and left space for more information.

"Simplicity means living simply and sharing your gifts with others. Stewardship means using the earth and its resources only to the extent you need them, and sharing the resources under your stewardship with all."

"The Friendship Train is sharing our gifts with others," I said.

"The other two, peace and education, have caused some problems for Quakers. Since we believe in peace, we don't believe in bearing arms against our fellow man. Instead of fighting in World War I, I signed up with the American Friends Service to do rehabilitation work in Serbia, a country devastated by war."

"The peace belief might not be popular when other people are getting killed." I thought Mr. Gaston might not like Mr. Pearson or his Quaker beliefs.

"It isn't. Quakers have wrestled with allegiance to country and allegiance to their faith for years, and our views on education aren't always popular either." Mr. Pearson had a far away look in his eyes.

"Why? I'd think everyone would be for education."

"Well, Quakers think both religious and secular education should be offered to women as well as men."

"My friend Margaret should go to college 'cause she's really smart," I told him.

"I hope Margaret will go to college." He changed his tone, "I predict one day we will have a woman president."

I laughed, and Mr. Pearson patted me on the back because I'd caught his joke. He closed each radio broadcast with news predictions and he had an 85-to-90% accuracy rating. Listeners wrote down his predictions and confirmed his correctness when the President or Congress acted the way he'd foretold.

My stomach growled, and Mr. Pearson pointed to my midsection and suggested I feed the lion. I liked Mr. Pearson, but he wouldn't be the one to help me capture the bad guys, since he had just told me he believed God lived in everyone. This confused me, because Mr. Pearson's main business was exposing bad guys.

If I chose Samuel for my detective sidekick, he might lose his job, and if he got fired, his daughters wouldn't go to college. If they didn't go to college, they wouldn't have careers, and their dreary lives would be my fault. I needed lunch and some thinking time.

After my egg salad sandwich and banana, I stood between the cars where I'd seen Mr. Pew and Mr. Gaston last night. Seeing how quickly the train raced through the flat Nebraskan landscape made me dizzy. Today, Nebraska, Thursday, Iowa, Friday, Illinois. I couldn't save the train by myself, I needed help. I walked forward and found Papa and Mr. Pew whittling the whistles Papa gave to the kids at train stops.

"How's my boy?" Papa asked.

"Doing good. You ready for lunch? I already ate, but I could sit with you, if you're hungry."

"I'll take you up on your offer. Thomas, want to join us?"

Mr. Pew waved us away with his huge hand. He was really big and really scary. When Papa and I cleared the first car, I blurted out my news.

"Papa, Mr. Pew and Mr. Gaston are planning to blow up the Friendship Train in Chicago. We have to stop them."

Papa grabbed both my shoulders and turned me squarely to face him. "What are you talking about?"

"I've heard them planning, two different nights," I explained everything I knew.

Papa sized me up, the way he did when he bought something expensive. He put his left hand over his mouth and breathed heavily through his nose. He didn't say a word.

"I'm...I'm...I am telling the truth, Papa."

"Jimmy, I'm afraid your imagination is working overtime. Thomas Pew is a fine man. He's big, and his face will never win a beauty prize, but he's a good man."

My mouth fell open in what Billy and I called the fly-catching mode. Papa always believed me, and now he believed in Mr. Pew rather than the proof his own son had given him.

"Got your speech ready for the next stop?" Papa nudged me to continue our walk toward the dining car.

Why had Papa changed the subject? Why had Papa ignored the truth? I never expected to have to save this train all by myself. Where were my detective sidekicks when I needed them most?

THIRTEEN

I sat with Papa in the dining car, but I made poor company, silently watching him eat a bacon and cheese sandwich. He offered me the pickle slice, but I shook my head. Mr. Pearson scheduled me to speak in Grand Island, but my somber mood didn't fit with cheering crowds, bands, and excitement. I wanted to take a nap, but only babies nap, so I slumped in a chair and waited.

The Friendship Train averaged six stops a day and the train travelers' eagerness bubbled up in spurts, like coffee gurgling into a percolator's glass top. Smiles broadened and the laughter flowed long before we reached the depot and saw the waiting food cars. Then the crowd's love and excitement lifted our spirits even higher.

After a stop, everyone on the train talked louder and faster, just like our baseball team did after a victory. Those guys would understand this craziness, because after a win, we went over each inning, play by play, and we felt like every kid on the team was our best buddy. We laughed and yelled and wanted to hug each other — but settled for arm punching and backslaps instead.

The music and cheers got louder as we approached Grand Island, and I trudged to the gathering spot so I could do my duty. The crew set up the gondola car with lights, microphones, and cameras, and Mr. Pearson greeted the community representatives and posed for pictures. I think the man had a clock in his head, because after a short time, he signaled the local master of ceremonies to begin.

I'd learned to enjoy giving talks and I'd even considered becoming a politician. I usually felt keyed up about speaking, but not today. Papa hadn't believed me. The heavy burden of the train's fate rested on my shoulders. When Mr. Pearson pulled me toward the microphone, I realized I'd been woolgathering and missed half the ceremony.

I'd forgotten everything I'd said at earlier stops, so I pulled out my harmonica and played *Over There*, not in the chipper, fast way, but in a slow, melancholy way. After I finished, the silent crowd waited. I talked, but what came out wasn't one of my usual speeches.

"Over there, in France" I began, "my brother Johnny, made friends. A family like mine, like yours, helped him avoid capture by the Nazis, and Johnny returned to the battlefield to fight for our freedom before he died."

Silence. Even babies and toddlers stopped squawking.

"Over there," I said, "that family is now fighting a war—a war to survive. Over here, we have food shortages and meatless days, but we have food. Thank you for giving so that the people who helped soldiers, like my brother, can live."

I stepped back into my spot. Nobody clapped. The master of ceremonies didn't move. I'd ruined the whole day. I should have told them I had a sore throat and couldn't talk. After what seemed like two or three years, Mr. Welsh moved to the microphone and sang slowly in his strong baritone voice.

Over there, over there,
Send the word, send the word
Over there
That the food is coming,
The food is coming,
From over here to over there.

After he finished, the drummer did loud rat-a-tat-tats, and the band started the same song with an up tempo. The master of ceremonies tapped his shiny black shoes to the beat, and when the band finished, he moved to the microphone and saved the day I'd almost destroyed.

The mayor affixed the sign labeled "From Grand Island, Nebraska" to the boxcars and the high school glee club closed the program with the national anthem. Embarrassed, I rushed to get back inside the train, but people kept handing me money. Before I left the platform car, both the pockets in my pants and coat jingled with coins.

Mr. Pearson slipped his arm around my shoulder. "Jimmy, your words tonight came straight from the heart."

"I thought I'd messed things up."

"No, you showed us the train's real mission."

The cash donations totaled more than we'd had from other stops, and church-like gratitude replaced the happy backslapping feeling we usually felt.

Samuel inquired about dinner, and the group decided to eat after Fremont and before Omaha, the last Nebraska stop. Samuel served drinks and offered snacks.

Miss Canty tapped her glass. "Henri Bonnet, the Ambassador from France, will be joining the train for the Omaha and Council Bluffs stops."

"Hear, hear." The people in the club car cheered and lifted their glasses in a toast.

I couldn't share their pleasure because this train moved too fast. We'd sleep in Iowa tonight.

A sharp poke in my back caused me to flinch. Mr. Gaston grinned and gave a deep-throated chuckle sounding like a creature from a horror movie.

"Scare you? Where's the big man who wanted to know about the war and how to blow things to smithereens? I thought you were going to bawl like a sissy little girl at our last stop."

I bit my lip, because I really wanted to give him a knuckle sandwich, but Mama and Papa taught all us kids to be respectful to adults.

"Cat got your tongue?" Mr. Gaston jabbed me gently with both fists like a boxer and flexed his fingers in a come-on motion, encouraging me to take a swing at him.

"Nah. I'm just tired." I yawned to prove my words and backed away. He acted like a bully. Maybe adults aren't any different than kids, just bigger. Mr. Gaston wouldn't get new friends to replace his pals killed in the war if he acted like a jerk all the time.

"Don't get huffy. I'm kidding. Want me to buy you a soda pop?"

"No, thanks. I'm not thirsty."

I don't think I'd ever turned down a free soda in my life, and Mr. Gaston looked disappointed. I should have taken his offer and pried more information from him, but I couldn't. If he felt lonely, he could stay lonely. I wasn't going to be his friend.

I wondered if Mr. Gaston behaved differently before his friends died. Maybe he and his mean bully friends stuck together because nobody liked them. Did I act like Mr. Gaston when I teased Margaret? I didn't like that idea. Margaret had told me I was always mean to her. I'd talk to Billy about the way we treated Margaret when I got home. I didn't want anyone to think I was like Mr. Gaston, even Danny Metz.

My head hurt. I didn't understand why Mr. Gaston enjoyed scaring me, why Mr. Welsh liked helping me, why Mr. Pearson liked teaching me, or why I'd been mean to nice Margaret Allen.

In our compartment, I scratched out another letter to Billy and got things straight in my mind. I confessed I'd never be a secret agent or a crackerjack detective. I could picture Billy nodding to indicate his understanding. I wrote about Mr. Welsh saving the day, Mr. Pearson complimenting me, and how much Papa's not believing me hurt. I felt lucky to have a good, true friend.

I hid Billy's letter in my suitcase. I couldn't risk someone reading the detective information I'd told him. Maybe I'd keep the letter and read my words to Billy when I got home. I pictured us sitting at the Parker kitchen table gobbling up his mom's peanut butter cookies.

I sure missed Mrs. Parker's cookies. She mashed down the peanut butter cookie dough with a fork before she baked them. She didn't smash down any other cookie type. I retrieved Billy's letter and added a P.S. asking why his mother did the thing with the fork on peanut butter cookies. Then I hid my letter again.

I pulled out a comic book Samuel had given me and thought about Tarzan fighting diamond smugglers in the African jungles. The rhythm of the wheels slowed. Could two and a half hours have passed? After Fremont, we ate dinner, and I'd scarcely finished my meatloaf before the conductor announced Omaha.

Mr. Henri Bonnet, the French Ambassador to the United States, received loud applause when Mr.

Pearson introduced him. Mr. Bonnet showed surprise at the food gathered and expressed his gratitude.

"You must be very proud," Ambassador Bonnet said, "as only communities formed of free citizens can do this. I can see these gifts are from individuals."

Tonight Mr. Pearson had a special announcement. "Earlier today, we confirmed the American Export Lines will carry at least half and maybe all the food to Europe without charge. This train's food will impact French and Italian lives, just as the giving of gifts is impacting American citizens and industries."

Nebraska crowds cheered, and we were on our way to Council Bluffs. Soon, the bright beams from the searchlights lit the darkness and a band played the *Iowa Corn Song*. The fire department focused its floodlights on their waiting boxcars. I shivered in the 20 degree temperature, stuck my gloved hands into my pockets, and stomped my feet to keep warm. Mr. Pearson acted like he didn't feel the cold, but he kept his speech short.

The dignitaries left for their comfortable hotel beds, and Papa and I went to the club car for some hot chocolate to get rid of the chill. I warmed my hands on the cup, and then touched my nose and cheeks with alternate hands to try and warm them too.

"Jimmy, I'm going to give half of Mama's money to Ambassador Bonnet to deliver to the Deschamps."

"What about the other half?" I sipped my hot chocolate.

"I'll give the other to Mr. Pearson in New York. He's going to France."

"Fine with me." Why Papa was talking about his money belt again?

"Adults must think about options, and carrying all this money makes me a little uncomfortable. Jimmy, you're growing older and wiser every day, and if anything should happen to me..."

"Are you afraid someone might rob you?"

"No. Now, if anything happens," Papa continued, "you can count on Samuel."

"Papa?"

"I'm just thinking out loud. We're pretty far from home, and Mr. Pearson and Miss Canty are busy with a million details in getting this trip to a successful conclusion. Our politician and railroad friends are also busy. If you need help, talk to Samuel."

"Papa?"

Papa didn't answer. He tousled my hair and bent toward me. I thought he kissed my head, but I probably imagined it, 'cause men don't go around kissing. His touch should have comforted me, but my jittery stomach told me Papa was worried about something—something he didn't want to tell me.

He should have told me, because no matter how big his worries, they were probably smaller than the horrible things my imagination invented.

FOURTEEN

My nightmares continued after I woke up. Did Papa want to run away? Maybe seeing the country made him want to travel. Maybe he missed Mama so much he wanted to take a vacation from work and from me. He probably didn't like worrying about me. I'd kept him informed about my whereabouts after Reno like I'd promised, but how lost could a kid get on a fast-moving train?

What if Papa had a horrible disease and only a few weeks to live? What if he had polio like Roosevelt had or cancer or a heart problem? If Papa died, I'd live with Martha, her husband and the twins. Their crammed apartment was bursting at the seams, and those twins liked to get into my stuff. I never found my favorite baseball card after they'd torn through my room this past summer.

Living with Martha and keeping my eyes on two little kids would be tough. I'd have to sleep on the couch, and hide my special collections. Maybe Billy would store some important things at his house, except

I liked having the things I saved near me. They were a part of me.

A third possibility was that scary Mr. Pew had gained power over Papa and talked him into doing something horrible like robbing a bank where Papa might get killed. Then I'd officially become an orphan — in Iowa, or Illinois, or Indiana, or wherever. The police would put me in an orphanage, and I'd never see my sister or Billy again. I'd have to work all the time, and I'd never get to practice baseball, and I'd never become a famous baseball player.

My thoughts circled like a toy train following the track around a Christmas tree, pausing at each horrible scene in my future. I couldn't break the pattern my mind followed, and the imagined possibilities grew more terrible with each lap of my future prospects.

The night Mama died, when my parents had their disagreement, Papa told her he was disappointed because she'd kept a secret from him. He said they didn't keep secrets because they loved each other. Well, shouldn't Papa's rule about secrets apply to his kid too?

I worried all night and into morning, but after I recalled Papa's speech about secrets, I got mad, really mad. Papa himself noticed I was growing up. If Papa wanted to dump me and go see the country, or go to a hospital, or even go rob a bank, well, he could just go. But he should tell me. I deserved the truth!

I stalked down the aisle, mad as a wet hen, to meet the others for the Ames, Iowa stop.

"Mr. Jimmy," Samuel stopped me. "I've been looking for you. I found some tokens from a past run and they're good for free drinks from the Ames Drugstore soda fountain."

"Uh, oh, thanks, Samuel."

"You're wearing quite a long face today. Is everything okay?"

"Everything's wonderful," I lied and forced a smile. "Thanks for the tokens. Do you think I'll have time to use them?"

"I think so, and you might find something else to interest you. The Ames drugstore carries all the latest comics."

Samuel's gift brightened my day. I liked my cola with chocolate and lemon. Billy always chose either cherry or vanilla. He never mixed flavors. Most Saturdays, after Billy and I went to the movies, we stopped at the drugstore, got a drink, and checked out the latest comics. I tucked the tokens into my pocket and planned to skedaddle immediately after the session.

At the Ames stop, kids waved autograph books for signatures, sang, giggled, and picked on one another. Riding with adults made me feel important, but I missed my friends.

I wanted to talk to someone my own age about what I saw for the first time—the mountains capped with snow, the thick trees, the Great Salt Lake, and the flat plains. Any kid, even Danny Metz, would have been impressed.

Maybe I was homesick. In one letter from France, Johnny wrote he was homesick. He hungered for Mama's cooking, Papa's jokes, and sitting at the dinner table with us. He also missed the ocean's smell, the thick vanilla malts from the drugstore, and watching movies with his friends. I guess homesickness is missing the things you've always had, but never think about.

I took my regular place on the platform next to Papa, but I did not stand close to him because I was mad at him for keeping secrets. He took a step closer to me, and I took two side steps to be further from him, making a spot for the Iowa governor.

Governor Robert Blue added his name to the big scroll all governors signed and began his welcome speech. "The people of Iowa are extending the hand of friendship to the hungry people across the sea. Our hope is they catch the spirit of this great state and our nation."

Mr. Pearson said he hoped every farmer had included their picture and their name and address in the grain sacks they'd donated, so I talked about the letters and maps we'd put in the milk cases. When I mentioned that Margaret had written a letter in French, some girl in the audience yelled that she'd written her letter in Italian. That Iowa girl was probably a teacher's pet too.

After the speeches, workers began loading, labeling, and connecting boxcars. I snapped a few pictures and told Papa about Samuel's tokens.

"I might be able to join you, if you can wait a few minutes," Papa said.

"You don't have to. I won't get lost. You can see the drugstore from here."

I kept my tone respectful, but I think Papa figured out I was angry at him for not believing me. He didn't act like he was mad at me. In fact, he winked and waved me off, and his mouth corners turned up ever so slightly.

A perfume, medicine, and hamburger scent mixture hit me when I opened the drugstore door, the same smell our drugstore at home had. The black countertop for the soda fountain made a backward L, and six-seater wooden booths decorated with carved initials filled the back of the store.

I hopped on a red vinyl revolving stool on a chrome base and twirled around and around, glimpsing my face each time in the big mirrored wall behind the neatly stacked pyramids of glasses and ice cream dishes. Whirling past, I noticed nut and cherry containers and bananas in a bowl, waiting to be changed into banana splits.

I'd only had one banana split in my whole life and the concoction was so delicious I'd eaten every bite, but my stomach sure ached that night. This drugstore had the same familiar green malt mixing machines lined up and ready for action. I felt like I was home.

"Slow down, young man. We don't want you twisting the stool so many times you dig a hole to China." The pleasant-faced man tied his apron and rolled up his shirt sleeves before continuing. "Aren't you the boy from the train?"

"Yes. How did you know?"

"Well, I know most youngsters here, and you look like the young man Mr. Pearson called Jimmy Burns. Can I get you something?"

"Is this worth a chocolate lemon coke?" I offered the wooden circle.

"You bet." The aproned man grabbed a pull-out nozzle, and sprayed cola over the ice.

Flavors marked the pump tops of the silver-colored containers, each with a pointy dispenser resembling a giant bird beak. The man pressed the chocolate button all the way down, and the brown gooey syrup oozed into my glass. He followed with a lemon squirt and stirred my drink with a teaspoon.

I'd pulled a wrapped straw from the tall cylinder on the counter and removed the end of the paper. I usually blew the covering across the room, but I was on my best behavior. I sampled my chocolate and lemon cola and sighed contentedly.

"Jimmy, I'm curious. Where'd you get the wooden nickel?"

"A wooden nickel?" I stared at the token he held.

"Haven't seen one in six months or so."

A wooden nickel? How many times had Billy warned me not to take wooden nickels? A hundred? A thousand? A million? The saying was a joke between us, but a wooden nickel could bring bad luck. I sucked on the straw until a loud glurping sound signified my glass was empty. I needed to leave before something horrible happened.

"Train porter gave it to me." I offered the counter man my second token, eager to get away. "Thanks for the drink."

I'd just pushed the glass toward him and slipped off the stool, when I recognized a deep, ugly voice.

"How about three burgers and three chocolate malts?" Mr. Gaston's low voice boomed.

I scooted behind the double-sided magazine rack and pretended to be very interested in a *Ladies' Home Journal.*

The patties sizzled when they hit the grill and the counter man filled a metal container with malt ingredients and hooked the frosty tin on the green mixer. The machine whirred noisily, and I sneaked a look at Mr. Gaston and the two strangers. Using the malt machine noise to cover my movements, I inched to the magazine rack's end so I could eavesdrop.

"Did you get ammonium nitrate for your crops?" Mr. Gaston asked.

The two men grinned like he'd told a great joke.

"Yes, indeedy. I like to put mine in 20-gallon gasoline containers," a man with a wide gap between his front teeth said. "Then sometimes, for fun, I pour fuel oil over the ammonium nitrate."

"Walls have ears, you know," Mr. Gaston said, giving a deep throaty laugh.

The aproned man placed the burgers and malts on the counter. "Here you go. If you don't need anything else, I'll be stocking in the pharmacy. Just give a whistle when you're ready for the check."

Those three went after the burgers like they hadn't eaten in a week.

"We got something else, too." the tall skinny man slurped on his malt. "We were afraid we might have an accident or a flat tire, so we got several flares. They burn real hot, you know."

The comment made them all laugh. I stood petrified, too frightened to write.

"Got some help on the train, too." Mr. Gaston bragged. "We decided Sterling, Illinois could use some excitement, before the train splits in Chicago. You can drive your pick-up to Sterling with the stuff in the back and park in the depot lot. When the train gets in, we'll meet you. Nobody suspects a man carrying a gasoline can, and we can stick the flares in our pockets."

"I want to be far away when those cars blow," Mr. Gap-tooth said.

"Don't worry. Flares burn bright when you break them, but we'll be long gone before anything happens." Mr. Gaston grabbed a toothpick and worked on his upper front teeth.

"We're just wrecking the cars, right? We won't be killing people, will we?" The tall skinny man wanted assurance.

"Nah, we won't hurt anyone," Mr. Gaston promised. "I'll mail an anonymous letter to the newspaper so people will understand why this food should stay in America."

"You paying for the burgers?" the skinny man asked.

"Paying for one, that's all I ate." Mr. Gaston gave a whistle to get the counter man's attention.

My heart sank. I had to get their picture. I stepped from my hiding place and acted shocked to see my old pal, Mr. Gaston. I raised my camera and snapped their picture before they had a chance to move.

"Hey, Mr. Gaston. You know, being in this drugstore is like being home." I took a couple more pictures of the drug store itself so they wouldn't be suspicious. "I had a chocolate lemon cola, and I've been checking out Tarzan's latest adventures. See you on the train."

I forced myself to walk slowly, even though my feet wanted to run the 100-yard dash. I lollygagged long enough to shoot their Ford pickup with my camera. I tried to include the license plate, but my snapshot might be blurry because my hands were shaking.

I'd done a very brave thing photographing the train saboteurs and I'd fooled them completely. The Hardy Boys had nothing on me. I'd solved this case all by myself.

I knew *who* was involved. I knew *what* was going to happen, *when* the bombing would happen, and *why* they were planning to blow up the train. I even knew *how* they were making the bombs. For positive proof, I'd taken the men's pictures and photographed the pickup to be used for transporting the bomb stuff.

My proud feeling didn't last the walk to the train. Who would believe me? Mr. Pearson thought my spy work was a game. Papa didn't trust me, and he might be leaving soon to start his traveling or hospital stay or bank robbing career. My pictures only showed three men at a soda fountain and a parked pick-up. No one heard their conversation except me.

Back on the train, I asked a photographer if he'd get my pictures developed at the Cedar Rapids stop. Getting pictures wasn't a problem, time was. We'd stop overnight in Clinton, Iowa, but we'd be in Sterling, Illinois at noon tomorrow. I shuddered. How on earth could one thirteen-year-old kid save the Friendship Train?

FIFTEEN

Watching Iowa zoom past the window, I remembered the verse from Psalm 46 that our Sunday School teacher recited every week—*God is our refuge and strength, a very present help in trouble.*

Well, trouble surrounded me, and I certainly needed help, strength, and maybe even a place to hide. I hadn't been so good about praying lately, and I hoped God would remember me. I slipped into our compartment to talk to God with thoughts, not words, because I didn't want a passerby to hear me mumbling about bombing the Friendship Train.

I put my elbows on my knees, rested my chin on my fists, and closed my eyes. *God, it's me, Jimmy. First, I'm sorry I haven't been regular about my prayers, and I plan to do better, but right now, I'm in big trouble.*

I started to tell God everything and stopped. God knew. *God, I need help to stop Mr. Pew, Mr. Gaston, and his pals from bombing the train. I've been kinda mean to Papa 'cause he didn't believe me and I'm sorry. Anyway, could You give me a sign—not anything big, like a burning bush — but something to let me know what to do. Thanks. Amen.*

I waited for probably five minutes and nothing happened, so I went to check on my film I mentally repeated the verse from Psalms in rhythm to my steps walking to the club car. *God is our refuge and strength, a very present help in trouble.* Trouble ended up being two steps, *trou* and *ble*, and I stomped those two syllables.

By the time I reached the train's activity hub, I'd said the verse about ten times and felt much better. Samuel saw my last two loud clomps, but smiled like my stomping walk was natural.

"Samuel, thanks for the tokens. I got a chocolate lemon cola, and you were right about the drugstore being interesting."

I offered my hand to Samuel, and he beamed. The train porter would never know the interesting thing about the drugstore happened to be a bomb plot to destroy this train. The club car buzzed with conversation, with Mr. Pearson's voice rising above the others.

"Illinois seems to be the heart, so Sterling might be a dangerous spot," Mr. Pearson said.

My ears perked up when I heard Mr. Pearson using words straight from my uneasy mind.

"Is Sterling dangerous?" I asked, trying to sound calm.

"When we mapped our route, we thought we might meet resistance in Illinois, the isolationist cradle."

"Yeah. Those isolationists can be trouble." I stroked my chin and tried to look thoughtful. I didn't want Mr. Pearson to think he'd selected a complete dunce for the train.

"Isolationists don't want to be involved in world problems, but we are a part of the world." Mr. Pearson rolled his head in a circle and we all heard his neck crack.

"The men in Utica, New York who stole the cases of evaporated milk from the train donations claimed to be isolationists," Mr. Welsh said. "When they got caught, they declared they deserved the milk more than the people in Europe."

Wow. I coughed to keep from laughing as I thought of another mystery book I could write, *The Case of the Evaporating Milk.* Billy would love that title since our school collected cases of evaporated milk.

"Isn't it strange for Americans to be isolationist when we're all immigrants?" Mr. Welsh looked around the car. "I bet every man here could name the country his family came from."

"I hope we're wrong about our concerns," Mr. Pearson said. "We feared the reception in the Midwest would be lukewarm, but Iowa has been incredibly generous, adding twenty-two cars. I believe the feeling will continue in Illinois."

Mr. Pearson sounded confident. But why had he mentioned isolationists and Sterling? Did he know something? I couldn't think about that. I had my own anxiety list. Papa used to tell Mama that worry never put bread on the table or solved a single problem, so I abandoned my worries about what my pictures might or might not prove, and flipped open my notebook.

My newspaper story flowed. I wrote about the kids in Ames and the visit to the drugstore—not about Mr. Gaston and his friends—but about how Ames and Oakland were alike. I included the stolen milk story and explained isolationism.

Miss Canty and Mr. Pearson made changes and corrections. Mr. Pearson suggested the theft be omitted and said issues of isolationism needed more space than the newspaper allotted for my report. After my third rewrite, Miss Canty approved the story.

"Ambassador Bonnet is joining us again in Chicago," Miss Canty said. "He's so grateful for the donations collected for France, he wanted to fly out for a second visit."

"Maybe he just likes to ride in planes." I responded. "I'd sure like to see this country from the air. You ever been in an airplane, Miss Canty?"

"Yes, and the view is amazing. Puffy clouds surround you and down below the rivers, highways, farms, and towns look like tiny toy train villages. I'll make a prediction on Mr. Pearson's behalf and say you'll get to ride in an airplane some day, Jimmy."

"I will," I said confidently. "I might even become an airplane pilot."

"You could, after your baseball career." Miss Canty's eyes sparkled.

She might have been teasing me, but I didn't care. I really could be a pilot. Johnny parachuted from airplanes, and I'd rather fly a plane than jump out of one. Then Mr. Gaston's face flashed in my mind. I might not survive to be an adult, much less have two or three careers. I pushed his leering mug from my memory and concentrated on copying my story.

The crowd at Greene Square in Cedar Rapids pushed to get a closer look at the train and to hear all the speakers. Local representatives presented seven cars of oats and over $7,000 in contributions.

"We never thought we'd have eighty-one cars by the time we reached Chicago," Mr. Pearson told the cheering crowd, "but the compassionate Iowans exceeded our expectations."

The mayor told about a local farmer. "Mr. Olson sold a team of work horses and gave all the money to the Friendship Train. His gift exemplifies Iowa's benevolent spirit."

Papa and I both spoke, and I let Papa stand close to me and didn't shrug when he rested his arm on my shoulder. Being mad at Papa felt wrong. Even though he hadn't believed me about Mr. Pew and Mr. Gaston, he'd been a great father over the years, so I chose to be nice to him.

Gazing into the crowd, I thought about my prayer request and wondered if I'd recognize God's sign. I just hoped the signal wouldn't have anything to do with arithmetic, because if God sent a math sign, I'd miss it for sure. But God knew all about my trouble with figures, so surely He wouldn't do that to me.

We waved good-bye to Cedar Rapids, and the train chugged toward Clinton, the overnight stop. Tomorrow morning, our schedule would be: Clinton, Iowa at 10:30; Sterling, Illinois at 12:10; Mr. Gaston and the bombs at 12:15. I wished I could stop time.

I prayed a reminder request to God, just in case He'd been busy with a bigger problem earlier. I don't understand how God can listen to prayers from all over the world, in different languages, at the same time, and give each the right answer. I should start listing all my questions on a tablet, because my head couldn't hold them all.

"Got your pictures," the photographer nudged my arm with an envelope. "I took a look at your work. You've got some blurry ones. To keep that from happening, hold your breath when you push the button. Slightest motion, even breathing, can blur your shot."

"Thanks for the hint. How much do I owe you?"

"My paper will cover it. See you later, Jimmy."

I looked at my Friendship Train journey in pictures. My shots of Mr. Pew and Papa coupling cars were great, but my drugstore photograph only showed Mr. Gaston, Gap-Tooth and Skinny having lunch. I wanted to make little balloons above their heads and fill them with the words I'd heard spoken. My detective pictures were worthless.

We arrived in Clinton about midnight, a time I'd normally be fast asleep, but tonight I felt wide-awake and energetic. I helped Miss Canty get her luggage to the taxi, and noticed Mr. Pearson and a red-haired man in serious conversation. Mr. Pearson placed his hand on the man's arm in a warning gesture when I walked toward them.

"Jimmy, shouldn't you be sleeping? We want you awake for tomorrow." Mr. Pearson chuckled.

Why couldn't people forget about the *one* time I fell asleep in the closet in Reno? They always remembered the night I wanted to forget.

"Samuel lent me his alarm clock, sir. I'll be awake for the program."

"I know you will. Jimmy, this is Daniel Helpher, the Clinton police chief."

"Helper? You're Mr. Helper?"

I gawked open-mouthed at God's obvious answer to my prayer.

"It's actually spelled H-e-l-p-h-e-r, the *ph* in the middle is pronounced like an *f,* but I answer to Helper too." The man wearing the black wool topcoat offered me and Mr. Pearson his hand. "Glad to have you folks in town. Let me know if there's anything I can do for you."

"All I need is a bed." Mr. Pearson grabbed his suitcase and moved toward a taxi.

"Mr. Helper, I mean Mr. Helpher, you can do something for me and the Friendship Train because God sent you."

"Really?"

"Really. I asked God for a sign, and here you are."

Mr. Helpher scratched his thick red hair. "God sent me out at midnight to meet this train? I'll have to tell this story to the wife. Jimmy's your name, isn't it?"

"Jimmy Burns. You're here at midnight, and I'm awake, and your name is the sign you're God's man."

"How about telling me the whole story over some hot cocoa?"

"Swell, but I have to let Papa know where I'm going." I ran toward the train.

"Invite him." Mr. Helpher yelled after me.

I didn't invite Papa, but I did promise him I'd be quick. I snatched the picture envelope and rushed back to Mr. Helpher.

Knowing our time limits, my words gushed out. I gave him the full scoop with all the *w's* and the *h* of Mr. Gaston and Mr. Pew's plan to blow up the train. I showed him Mr. Gaston, Gap-Tooth and Skinny in the drugstore picture and Mr. Pew's picture coupling cars. I pushed the pickup photograph toward him and apologized for the license plate's blurriness.

The police chief studied me, took a swig of his cocoa, and eyed me again with a penetrating gaze almost as intimidating as Mr. Pearson's, but I matched the red-haired man's stare and didn't blink.

"Have you told anyone about this?"

"I tried to tell Papa, but he didn't believe me about Mr. Pew. I didn't want to get Samuel involved, and Mr.

147

Pearson is very busy, so I asked God for help. He sent you. Every word I told you is the truth."

"I believe you. I pegged you for an honest and trustworthy young man right off the bat."

"Well, I'm not all good. Margaret, a girl in my class, told me I was mean, but I'm going to be nicer to her, and I have a temper, and I sometimes hold grudges, and . . ."

"Hold up. We all have our faults. I meant your basic character. May I borrow your photographs?"

I quickly slid the evidence to Mr. Helpher who lifted his cocoa cup in a salute. He believed me!

"I'll drive to Sterling tonight and set up a watch on the depot parking lot. I think stopping them before they put those explosives on the train would be a good idea, don't you?"

I nodded.

"Tomorrow, we'll need you to identify the men. Can you do that?"

I nodded again.

"Since you'll be on the platform, you can watch us make the arrest. I'll wear my bright green hat, clashes with this red mop." He pointed to his head. "You won't have any trouble spotting me. You're a courageous young man, Jimmy."

I skipped back to the train, feeling lighter than air. Papa grunted a groggy hello and goodnight when I climbed to the top berth. I didn't think I'd be able to sleep, but I never heard Papa's snoring, a sure sign I'd fallen asleep before he had. The next morning, I climbed down the ladder and shuffled quietly to the men's lounge with my clothes. Papa was still asleep when I got back.

"Rise and shine, Sleepyhead." I used the words Papa usually said to me and jostled his shoulder.

"Jimmy, I'm not feeling very well. Think you can handle the speeches in Clinton and Sterling?"

I thought he was teasing, but he didn't move. Papa never missed work, and I wondered if his tiredness might be the deadly disease's symptom. What if my nightmares did come true? What if Papa did have an incurable illness? What would I do without Papa?

"Sure. I'll make you proud." I tried to sound casual, but my voice tricked me.

"Don't worry, Jimmy. I'll be right as rain this afternoon."

After the Clinton presentation, I hurried to Papa and found him completely dressed, but still in bed.

"I think I'll be lazy and lay around all day today." Papa joked.

I didn't laugh. I sat with Papa listening to the train clickety-clack toward Sterling. I worried about Papa, but I wasn't worried about Sterling or the bombing, because God had provided a helper.

All the factories in the twin towns of Sterling and Rock Falls blasted their whistles to welcome the train. Scared, nervous, worried, and excited, I left Papa in the lower berth and made my way to the platform car.

From my vantage point, I had a clear view of the depot lot. Two police cars and an ambulance waited in the back row. Mr. Helpher, wearing his bright green hat, stood with six other men in the parking area's third row. Mr. Gaston's friend, the tall, skinny man, paced by his pick-up, and I knew Gap-Tooth would be nearby.

The police planned to move in when Mr. Pew and Mr. Gaston got to the truck. This beat watching an adventure movie. Skinny waved his hand toward the train. Three people emerged from between the train cars. Three people, not two, Mr. Pew, Mr. Gaston, and Papa.

What's going on? What was Papa doing with Mr. Pew and Mr. Gaston?

The band struck up a spirited *You're a Grand Old Flag,* and twelve men congregated at the truck filled with the explosive containers. Gap-Tooth ran, and Papa raced after him. In slow motion, I saw Mr. Helpher raise his gun and fire. Papa fell.

SIXTEEN

I couldn't breathe. The clapping, singing, and cheering sounded miles away and the actions in the parking lot happened in slow motion. I stared at the depot area, unable to move or speak.

Policemen handcuffed Mr. Pew, Mr. Gaston, and Skinny, and hustled them into a police car. Another man carefully moved the gasoline containers housing the home-made bombs to a brown van. Gap-Tooth, hands tied behind his back, received an escort to another police car.

Mr. Helpher waved his green hat, gave me a victory sign, and knelt over Papa who was being strapped on a stretcher. I prayed Mr. Helpher's bullet had missed Papa, but when they placed his big limp body on a stretcher, I saw the blood. Papa never moved when they lifted the stretcher into the ambulance.

What had I done? Was Papa dead? What kind of a kid was I? Was I under a curse? I hadn't told anybody about the hole in the path, and Mama tripped and died. Papa assured me Mama's death wasn't my fault,

151

and I wanted to believe him, but now I'd caused Papa to get shot. Something must be terribly wrong with me.

Why was Papa out there anyway? What was he doing with Mr. Gaston and Mr. Pew? What if Papa died too? Then I'd be responsible for both Mama's and Papa's death. I couldn't stay here. I had to get to Papa.

The band switched to *Yankee Doodle Dandy* and dancers, each one dressed as Uncle Sam, tapped their way from one side of the roped-off platform to the other. How could they play happy music when Papa might be dead?

I pushed my way behind the people on the platform car and ran through the aisles until I smashed into Samuel, knocking him off balance.

"Samuel, I need to get to the police station, now!"

Samuel never asked why; he just led me to the dining car where local grocery workers hoisted fresh fruits and vegetables to the train crew.

"This young man needs to get to the police station immediately. If someone can take him, I'll do that man's work." To indicate his intentions, Samuel jumped to the ground and reached for a lettuce crate.

The man in charge pointed a finger to a scrawny blond-haired boy whose jeans were rolled up three times and then to me.

"How far?" I asked.

"Six blocks or so." My guide started walking.

"Let's run. I need to get there fast."

He looked at me in surprise, but started to trot. We darted and dodged through the crowded streets and then he pointed to an old brick building with the words Police Department stenciled in the frosted glass over the door. I took the steps two at a time, then remembered to yell thanks to the boy before pulling open the heavy door.

"I need Mr. Helpher, the Clinton police chief." I gasped, tired from the six-block run. "It's about my father. It's very important."

The uniformed man behind the high wooden desk peered over his glasses. "Chief Helpher just got here himself, but he's pretty busy, son."

"I'm the one who told Mr. Helpher about the plot, then Papa showed up in the parking lot and Mr. Helpher shot him. Please, tell him Jimmy Burns is here and it's an emergency."

"That's a good story."

"It's not a story. It's the truth. Would you tell Mr. Helpher? Please!"

"Wait here. I'll see what he says. Jimmy Burns, right?" He eased from his chair and lumbered down the mint green hallway.

I followed, even though he told me not to. When the heavy man knocked, Mr. Helpher stuck his head out, listened, then glanced my way. The Clinton chief stepped into the hallway, and the desk clerk left.

"Jimmy. Good work! The local police say old Gap-Tooth and Skinny are singing like birds. I'm questioning Mr. Gaston, and the sergeant is working on Pew. The other fellow's in surgery, he bled a lot, but the doctors think he'll make it."

"He's alive? He's really alive? I couldn't believe you shot him." I slumped into a wooden bench by the wall.

"He ran. You saw him. You didn't show us his picture, but he came from the train with Pew and Gaston. You know him?"

"He's my papa," I said.

"Oh, son, I'm so sorry." Mr. Helpher sat beside me and patted my leg.

"You're sure he's not going to die?" I begged for a positive answer.

"The doctors said his odds were good. I thought you were brave before, having all this on your shoulders, but to know your own father had a part in this caper . . ."

I stopped Mr. Helpher. "He didn't. He wouldn't. I don't know why he ended up with them, but Papa's innocent."

"He'll get a chance to explain." Mr. Helpher paused. "I hate to say this, but your papa may not want to see you."

"He will. He will want to see me. I'm his boy." I breathed hard and sucked in as much air as I could grab.

"Your father will know his actions would embarrass and disappoint you." Mr. Helpher handed me a handkerchief dug from his pocket. "It's clean," he said. "Keep it."

"He'll tell you what really happened, and he will want to see me." I insisted, hoping to convince the police chief of Papa's innocence.

I'll take you to the hospital the minute they notify us your papa's operation is done. I won't be long with Mr. Gaston. You gave us all the information we needed."

"Can I stay with you?" I didn't want to be alone right now.

"Your call." He opened the door and I followed.

"Hello there. If it isn't little Jimmy, the Friendship Train's savior." Mr. Gaston bowed and applauded, and then leaned toward me, a sneer on his face. "You should be aware I have many friends, and I'll make sure every single one knows about you."

"That's enough, Gaston." Mr. Helpher shook his head in disgust.

Mr. Gaston laughed his evil laugh, pointed his finger at me and said, "Pow."

"I, I've changed my mind. I'll wait outside." I felt for the doorknob behind me. I didn't want to turn my back on Mr. Gaston.

"I won't be long with this weasel," Mr. Helpher promised.

In the hall, I stared at the pictures of wanted criminals on the department bulletin board. I studied them closely, in case one of them might be Mr. Gaston's friend and show up on the train. This day certainly hadn't turned out the way I'd imagined.

"Helpher." The uniformed man from the desk knocked on the door before sticking his head inside. "You're a popular man. First, the hospital called, and our bad guy survived surgery, but he won't wake up for another thirty minutes. Second, Sarge wants you to talk to Pew in Room 108, some problem with him."

"Thanks." Mr. Helpher came out. "I'm through here. Kindly escort Mr. Gaston to your finest cell. Oh, let Jimmy and me leave first. Gaston's one mean fellow. We don't need any more yapping or threats from him."

I matched Mr. Helpher's steps down the white tiled floor, stretching my legs to the aching point. I wondered what problems Mr. Pew had created. His picture hadn't appeared on any wanted posters, but maybe not every criminal's mug got posted. Maybe Mr. Pew was a recently escaped murderer or a lunatic on the loose, or maybe he'd beaten up a guard or two or three when he made his getaway from prison.

When Mr. Helpher opened the door to Room 108, Mr. Pew stood up. He wasn't handcuffed and no other policemen were in the room. He headed straight for me.

Jeez Louise. Would he throttle me with those monster-sized hands?

"Back away from the boy, Pew. I'm a good shot," Mr. Helpher pointed his gun at Pew's chest.

The giant man stopped moving.

"How's Robert Burns?" Mr. Pew asked.

156

"Alive. Surgery's over. Jimmy and I are on our way to the hospital. Sergeant said you wanted to talk, so talk."

Mr. Pew addressed me. "Jimmy, I'm really sorry about your dad. I needed back-up and knew I could trust your father."

I moved slightly behind Mr. Helpher who still held his gun, and spoke boldly. "My papa would never join your gang. Did you threaten to break his legs or kill me?"

Mr. Helpher pulled out a chair for me, the farthest one from Mr. Pew, and pushed down on my shoulder, forcing me to sit.

"Why don't you take a seat too, Mr. Pew. Tell us your side." Mr. Helpher remained standing.

"You can put the gun away. We're on the same side," Mr. Pew said.

"I think we'll hear your story first." Mr. Helpher kept his gun aimed at Mr. Pew.

"Your men have checked my papers and telephoned my boss. Not too many men match my description." Mr. Pew traced the pinkish scar down his left cheek. "I'm a railroad detective, hired to protect the Friendship Train."

"Some detective! Jimmy's the one who uncovered this plot." Mr. Helpher holstered his gun.

"Mr. Gaston approached me with his plan, and I acted interested. He'd tell me a little something each day," Mr. Pew said.

"Why didn't you tell the police?" Mr. Helpher asked.

"Gaston gave me tidbits of information, but the train's always moving. Telling police in Utah wouldn't have done any good if the bombing had been set for Nebraska. My instructions were to eliminate problems by myself. When I heard the final plan, I knew I needed help."

Mr. Pew's story, if true, explained a lot of things.

Mr. Pew turned to me. "I trusted your father completely. Anyway, I told Gaston that Robert wanted to be in on the bombing. Gaston's not too bright, the man never questioned why Robert would want to be involved in a cockamamie bombing scheme."

"I heard *you* talking about bombing the train."

"You're a smart one, Jimmy. Robert thought he'd convinced you to forget about that." Mr. Pew paused.

"I didn't forget."

"I know. Robert and I thought we'd have the three men and explosives delivered to local police within ten minutes. Instead, we ended up in a three-ring circus."

"Jimmy tipped us off to the whole plan. He showed us pictures of people involved, told us what explosives would be used, and where and when the attack would happen," Mr. Helpher said.

"We had two groups trying to do one job," Pew said. "Jimmy, I wish the bullet had hit me instead of your dad. Everything happened so fast. When the man ran, Robert instinctively chased him."

Mr. Pew's ugly face twisted with shame and regret, and for the first time, I saw a man, not a scary monster. I held out Mr. Helpher's handkerchief to Mr. Pew, but he shook his head.

Mr. Helpher glanced at his watch. "Pew, this boy needs to see his papa. Want to come with us?"

On the ride to the hospital, I thought about everything Papa and I would discuss on the way to Chicago. I'd listen carefully to the doctor's instructions, and I'd be caring for Papa for a change. I might even remind Papa he'd have to tell *me* anytime he wanted to go somewhere. The muscles in my face ached from the big grin I wore.

The mint green paint coating the police station walls also covered the hospital's interior, but the smells and sounds were different. Sweat, old newspapers, stale coffee, and loud voices made up the police atmosphere while the hospital smelled of disinfectant and flowers, and only the sound of a nurse's squeaky shoes broke the silence.

"Limit your visit to fifteen minutes. He needs rest," the nurse ordered.

The dim light showed a metal hospital bed cranked up about a third. White pillows and a white hospital gown framed Papa's pale face. I'd expected him to welcome us and retell his role in catching the criminals, but he lay still, eyes closed. I inched my way toward the bed and whispered his name.

"Jimmy." Papa reached for my hand.

Saying my name sapped his energy, so I talked. I've learned I talk a blue streak when I'm nervous, and my words tumbled out, filling the blank spaces housed by my fear for Papa's life. I told Papa about how God sent Mr. Helpher and how horrible I'd felt when Mr. Helpher shot him.

When I paused for a breath, Mr. Pew started. "I'm sorry, Robert. I never thought anyone would get hurt."

Mr. Pew almost touched Papa's shoulder, but pulled his hand back. Maybe he feared his big clumsy mitt would hurt Papa, or maybe Mr. Pew didn't want us seeing him act like a sentimental joe.

"I need to talk to Jimmy . . . privately." Papa whispered.

"We'll wait outside," Mr. Pew said.

The two adults eagerly left the room. From the time we walked through the front door, I could tell neither man liked visiting hospitals. I'd never been in a hospital before, and I didn't like being here either. I certainly didn't like seeing Papa look so helpless. My real papa joked, laughed, and lived with energy. This still, silent man with pain etched into lines on his face only looked like Papa.

"Jimmy, get my belt. It's with my clothes behind the curtain."

I tried not to look at the stain on his pants, but the blood stench filled the small closet. I struggled to remove the special belt filled with Mama's money from the stubborn loops.

"Here, Papa." I placed the belt on the edge of the bed.

"You're a skinny one, so it'll go around you twice. Put the belt next to your skin and then tuck your shirt in your pants." Papa never lifted his head off the pillow when he gave instructions.

"You should wear it, not me," I said.

"You're going on alone. Use Mama's money for anything you need and give the rest to Mr. Pearson in New York for the Deschamps."

"What if Mr. Pearson won't let me back on the train?"

"He'll be proud to have you. You saved the train. You're the best representative the American people could have."

"I can't leave you."

"Yes, you can. I'll rest up until you come back, and we'll go home together. Oh, you better use some money to give Martha a call."

I blinked my eyes several times to keep the tears in. I knew I should have a jillion questions, but I couldn't think of a one. I smoothed my shirt over the money belt, buttoned my coat and went back to Papa's bedside.

"Jimmy, can I count on you?"

Could he? I'd done so many things wrong, but Papa still believed in me. I couldn't let him down.

"Yes, you can." I stood a little straighter, determined to make sure Mama's dream and Papa's sacrifice to get food to our neighbors across the ocean would happen.

Mr. Helpher rapped on the door. "Sorry to interrupt, but the train's leaving in ten minutes. The boy might want to say good-bye to them," Mr. Helpher said.

"I'll be going on the train," I said with more confidence than I felt inside. "Papa and I represent the people of the United States. I'll finish the job we agreed to do."

"Thomas, make sure he gets on the train." Papa looked at his friend.

"Will do," said Mr. Pew. "Jimmy, the railroad's assigned another detective to the train. I'll stay with your papa until he gets back on his feet."

I held the metal bars on Papa's hospital bed, not wanting to leave him. I'd never been away from Papa for more than two days and then I'd been with Billy's family. Doubts crept into my mind. How could I go to the biggest city in the country all by myself?

"I'm proud of you, Jimmy. You'll be fine." Papa raked his fingers through my hair and then touched my cheek.

I gave Papa's hand a squeeze, squared my shoulders and walked out. I wanted Papa to believe I felt confident about finishing this journey, our personal mission to honor Mama.

I didn't turn around; Papa would have noticed that I was scared.

SEVENTEEN

Mr. Pew did the talking when we got to the train, giving me and Papa all the credit for foiling the train saboteurs. He didn't even mention being a railroad detective. I think Mr. Pearson knew, because he tilted his head and raised his eyebrows when Mr. Pew omitted his role.

I think every man on the train slapped me on the back to congratulate me. Some overly enthusiastic fellows whacked me pretty hard. A person could get hurt by well-wishers. I'd dreamed about being a hero, but this celebration felt hollow. Papa lay in a hospital bed, and Mr. Pew hadn't told the whole truth. I deserved some credit, but certainly not all.

Mr. Pearson halted the merriment. "Jimmy probably needs to catch his breath, and the rest of us have work to do. I've made two lists. One names those going on the New York route and the other lists those on the Pennsylvania run when this train splits in Chicago."

I sneaked off to my compartment. I knew I'd be staying with Mr. Pearson. Yesterday, I'd have been all ears, eager to learn who would stay on this train and who would be on the New York route with Henry Kaiser as honorary chairman. Today, I didn't care.

Samuel waited by our compartment. "Mr. Jimmy, would you like your dinner here this evening?"

"Yes. Thanks." Then mental alarm bells sounded. "Oh Samuel, you're not leaving, are you?"

"I'm staying on this run, but I'll get to see my family in Chicago. I was wondering if . . . if you have time, I'd like for my family to meet the fine young man who represents all Americans."

"Sure." I wanted to meet Samuel's girls, girls he planned to send to college.

Samuel said I represented *all* the people. I'd only thought about representing other kids like me, but without Papa, I'd act on behalf of all people, not just the kids. I'd speak for old people like Mrs. Martin who made great banana pudding; for people who moved to America, without speaking English, like the war brides; and people like Samuel who had different colored skin.

I spoke for people who seemed mean, like the clerk in Reno, and those who seemed nice, like the drugstore man in Ames. I served for the rich, like Governor Warren, and poor men in prison, who donated to the train. I was ambassador for the smart ones like Mr. Pearson, and even for little first-graders, who don't know anything.

Representing everyone weighed about two tons.

I moved my things to the lower berth and burrowed my face into Papa's pillow, savoring his Old Spice after-shave and engine-grease scent. The person who joined the train in Chicago could take the top berth — unless he was fat. I wouldn't want a fat man falling from the upper berth and breaking an arm or leg.

Smelling Papa's pillow made my eyes watery and itchy. Johnny cried when he went into the service. He didn't bawl like a baby, but a few tears sneaked down his cheeks. He'd represented America in a war and died. Papa represented America in peacetime, and he'd been shot.

Stinking, stinking wooden nickel! The thing put me in the wrong place at the wrong time. What I learned at the drugstore caused Papa to get shot. Now Papa suffered in a hospital, and I sat in the middle of North America, all by myself. I tried to sleep, but after flopping around like a fish on a line, I sat up.

I got money from Papa's belt for my phone call to Martha and wrote my newspaper article about how this train represented *all* the people. After my private dinner, I gave my story to Miss Canty. She scanned my work and handed the sheets to Mr. Pearson. For the first time, neither one suggested changes, so I prepared the pages to be telegraphed to Oakland.

Over 4,500 people waited at the North Western Terminal in Chicago to see their twenty boxcars attached. The Illinois governor, Dwight Green, received loud applause when he declared many first-generation Americans called Chicago their home.

"You know," Green pointed to the crowd, "the food on this train could help your own relatives abroad."

Speakers cut their talks short because separating the train and getting the cars to different terminals for a midnight departure would be time-consuming. The train cars going on the New York route had to be moved to the Central Terminal. The Pennsylvania route cars would be hauled to Union Station, while thirty-three cars would go directly to New York City to be loaded on barges for the Statue of Liberty salute.

During the shuffling, I traded dollars for change, found a phone booth, and called Martha's neighbor, because Martha didn't have a telephone. I heard a man yawn as he answered. I shifted my weight from foot to foot, willing him to hurry and get Martha because every minute he took ate into my talk time.

"Jimmy? What's wrong?" My sister sounded scared.

"Papa got shot and he's in a hospital in Sterling, Illinois."

"What?"

"I'm in Chicago and heading for New York. Papa said to call you. He didn't want you to worry. Good-bye."

"Do not hang up!" Martha yelled. "Now, you talk until the phone company cuts us off. How did Papa get shot? Is he going to live? Where did he get hit? Arm? A leg? The back?" Martha spoke with her bossy voice.

"Some men tried to blow up the train, and Papa and a railroad detective went to stop them. I'd heard about the plan and told the police. The police thought Papa and the detective were with the bad guys, who wanted to blow up the train, but they weren't, and then a bad man ran, and Papa tried to catch him and the police shot . . ."

The operator interrupted. "Your time is up. Please deposit additional coins or hang up."

"He'll live. Leg." I got the words out before the click ended our connection. I'd told Martha exactly what happened. Now she wouldn't worry. I left the phone booth in a great mood and went to find Samuel.

Wearing his spotless blue coat, our porter stood by the train with his family. Their clothes were starched and neat, the way Samuel himself always looked. I heard their happy laughter when I got closer.

"Here's Mr. Jimmy Burns, the people's representative. You heard him speak tonight. Jimmy, this is my wife, Claudine, and these are our daughters, Sarah, Esther, Vashti, and Deborah."

"Hello." My mind went blank, so I said hello again. How stupid can a person get?

"Mr. Jimmy loves baseball," Samuel said.

All their faces lit up like a roller blind had coiled up to let sunshine flood over them.

"I like the New York Yankees." My words darkened the light in their faces. "But I know you like the Brooklyn Dodgers, and I can cheer for the Dodgers—unless they play the Yankees." Now I was talking nervously. "Samuel says you're all going to college."

"So we've been told every day of our lives," said Sarah, who looked like a high schooler. "Esther and I want to be teachers, and Vashti plans to be a nurse. Don't stand still around her or she'll bandage your head or your arm. Vashti's operated on every doll in our house."

"I want to be a famous singer. Do you want to hear me?" asked Deborah.

"No!" Her three sisters answered in unison.

"Once she starts, you can't stop her." Esther explained the sisterly protests.

Since Deborah and I were both the youngest in our families, I knew how she felt.

I spoke right to her. "You've got a good name. The Deborah in the Bible was a brave, smart judge."

Deborah twisted back and forth and looked at her shoes.

"They all have names from the Bible." Samuel's wife pulled Deborah close to her. "We chose a princess, two queens and a judge. We wanted the girls to have strong names."

"And they're growing into strong young women." Samuel rested his hand on Vashti's head.

"Oh, Daddy," Vashti protested about her father's bragging on them, but I could see they all loved it.

"My parents chose Bible names for us too, a hard worker and three disciples—Martha, John, Andrew, and James, except they call me Jimmy."

"Those are great names. Are they all in California?" Samuel's wife asked.

"No. My brothers are dead, Johnny in the war and Andrew from the fever. But Martha and her husband live in Oakland and have twin boys."

I didn't want to tell Samuel's wife or these girls about Mama's death or Papa's being in the hospital, so I said I needed to get back to the train and left.

Samuel's family acted like we used to act. The kids teased each other, but you could see how much they liked each other, and they loved Samuel the same way I loved my papa.

I should have taken more money and talked to my sister longer. Martha would have fussed and given me advice, like Mama used to do. Martha had packed my clothes and helped me get ready for this trip. A million things I should have said to Martha passed through my mind, but I had a job to do.

I planned to watch the new people board and see if anyone resembled one of the criminals I'd seen on the police bulletin board. I wondered if I'd be able to identify either Mr. Gaston's friend or Mr. Pew's replacement. The detective would be undercover, so he'd be harder to spot.

A big-boned lady wearing a dark orange suit and a brown felt hat with two long pheasant feathers boarded first, and alone. I bet she wasn't a governor or mayor's wife—probably not anyone's wife, because she was ugly. Her long dished face looked like a horse's face, and in her high heels, she towered above all the men on the platform.

I considered her looks and her height to be two strikes against her in the marriage category, and if pretty Miss Rhodes couldn't get a man, this lady didn't have a prayer. Judging by her luggage, juggled by a huffing porter, she'd be changing clothes several times a day, so maybe she was trying to attract a husband.

"Emma Harkness is the name. I'm the new Voice of America reporter. My compartment number, please."

Her large voice matched her large frame, and since she didn't seem the patient type, I hoped her accommodations would be close. The poor porter struggled to get her bags through the narrow entry.

"You Jimmy?"

I jumped when a man wearing denims, a work shirt and tweed cap suddenly appeared. He spit out a black tobacco wad on the platform, just missing my right shoe.

"I am." I moved my foot, hoping he'd notice where he'd spit.

This cat-like man sized me up. Strange. The new lady had a horse face, and this man moved like a cat, sneaking up behind me without a sound. His greenish eyes and coal-black hair even made him look like a cat. He rounded his shoulders and stretched like he'd awakened from a nap.

"Call me Irish. Everybody does. In fact, not many people know I have a real name—I do, 'tis Tommy, but like I said, call me Irish. I'm bunking with you since your dad left the train."

"Oh."

"Don't say much, do you? That'll suit me fine, 'cause I can talk enough for both. Kissed the Blarney Stone, so they say. I'm the new railroad hand. Show me where to stow my kit."

He followed me to our compartment, and he talked the whole way. He told a joke about an Irish, a Frenchie and an Italian going to a pub. Then he had one about two sailors and an Irish man going to a pub, followed by a joke about an Irish priest going to a pub. After that, an Irish man and a duck, yes, a duck, going to a pub. I learned one thing from all his malarkey, the Irish are a lot smarter than other folks—folks in pubs anyway.

He hefted his bag to the top berth, and I didn't offer to trade. He wasn't fat and, if he fell, he'd probably land on his feet, like a cat.

"I don't sleep much," he said. "You need me to wake you for the stops?"

"No. You don't have to baby-sit me. I've been on this train for a whole week. Do *you* have any questions for me?" I asked.

He shrugged and started unpacking, yakking all the time. He wasn't the bunkmate I'd wanted. His jabbering grated on my nerves already. Maybe God wanted to teach me patience and to control my temper by sticking me with Irish. His blabbering caused me to miss seeing other people boarding, possibly bad guys sent by Mr. Gaston.

"I'm going to check on the loading and switching," I said, hoping for some relief from his constant chatter.

Instead, he draped his arm around my shoulder like we were best pals and started a story about an Irish man and his wife going to a pub. The next four days were going to be longer than normal, with him jawing non-stop. For a railroad man, Irish didn't seem too keen on learning how he could help.

Both trains left Chicago about midnight. Our train would stop at Fort Wayne, Indiana, but the ceremony wouldn't be until the next morning. I set Samuel's clock, so Irish didn't have to wake me. I thought I'd be uncomfortable without Papa, but I slept like a log until a soft metallic click caused me to wake.

I struggled to keep my breathing even and I opened my eyelids the tiniest bit. Through my lashes, I saw Irish sitting in the pull-down seat cleaning a pistol.

Jeez Louise. What next?

EIGHTEEN

Hearing a pistol cocked proved a more effective wake-up call than an alarm clock. I moaned and groaned a little, pretending to rouse from my night's sleep. A serious-looking Irish slid the gun into his pocket, eased the chair seat to the folded position, and slipped into the aisle. I watched him through half-closed eyes until he left, then my peepers snapped wide open.

My full bladder forced me to dance from one foot to the other, but I wanted to give Irish time to clear the corridor before I visited the john. I couldn't really think about my compartment companion, his gun, or what to do until I'd relieved myself. I checked the aisle — empty — and then raced to the men's lounge carrying my clothes with me.

Getting dressed, I wondered if Irish might be the detective. He'd talk to anybody, and he didn't sleep much. Those were good detective traits, but I didn't like the man. I'd guessed wrong about Mr. Pew, but Papa saw past Mr. Pew's ugly face and liked him immediately. Maybe when you got old enough to grow a mustache or beard, you judged a man's character more accurately.

In the dining car, I selected a table with a station house view showing the words Fort Wayne. I'd slept through our arrival, but the absence of noise and the empty seats told me the dignitaries had not returned from the hotel.

I ordered oatmeal and coffee with extra milk. Coffee drinkers could stay at a spot for hours without ordering anything else, and I hoped to see the people I'd missed last night when Irish chose to become my new best pal. My plan didn't work.

A high school band gathered, followed quickly by townspeople jostling each other to get a good spot for the ceremony. The faces blurred like they did when the movie reel broke and the film went too fast for your eyes.

The morning program felt a bit awkward to us regulars, because different people helped with set-up, and big Emma Harkness slowed us down as she presented one demand after another. Today she wore a dark green suit and a green hat — with two pheasant feathers. I wondered if she had pulled the feathers from the brown hat and stuck them in the green one.

Emma Harkness barked non-stop questions. "What equipment did the other reporter use? Could you hook that up for me? Where's the feed? How do I know when I'm on air? Explain the whole sequence to me. I want to get this right."

Her domineering tactics worked, and people jumped to answer her. Most questions seemed pretty basic, but then I'd been on the train for a week now, so I knew a lot.

The replacement train workers fell into their roles without any bumps, because they did the same thing on any train run. The new reporters, photographers, radio crews, and local dignitaries took longer to master their assignments and gauge the presentation's rhythm.

We'd added outsiders for short distances each day. Usually a mayor would join us at the stop before his city and governors often rode through the whole state. Both mayors and governors brought other people, people wanting to hear Friendship Train stories.

We insiders who'd been on the train all the way from California developed a Abbott and Costello type routine we played to our ever-changing audience of mayors, governors and food collection chairmen. However, with new people on board and old friends moved to the New York route, the timing and magic were missing.

The original crew tried to keep the attempted bombing, the arrests, and Papa's gunshot wound off-limits subjects, but the new riders hungered for every juicy tidbit. I knew when people were talking about *it* because silence fell when I got within earshot.

We only had a few stops today, so this would be a work day for the man in charge. Mr. Pearson's radio program would be broadcast from Altoona,

Pennsylvania tomorrow, and he'd promised I could watch. He wrote his *Washington Merry-Go-Round* syndicated column each day and broadcast his radio program each week even while running this huge project.

He received word each day about other train routes. The Southwest train promised 200 cars, hoping to outshine our cross-country journey, and the East and Southeast hoped to outdo the Southwest. Mr. Pearson focused on his work: pounding the Corona's keys, scribbling on pages, correcting papers, reading telegrams and newspapers, and requesting information from Miss Canty.

Once I'd touched Mr. Pearson's old typewriter, and he'd told me flat out he considered two things off limits to his staff--his office desk chair and his typewriter. The Corona rated special treatment because his father gave him the typewriter for graduation, and the journalist had traveled the globe with his gift, typing all his stories and articles on it. I knew his world stories had made him famous, but he didn't brag.

I wandered to the connecting platform between cars so I wouldn't be a bother and played all the songs I knew on my harmonica. I even made up a few, then went back to the club car and worked on my school journal, and the clock still didn't show time for lunch. Emma Harkness locked eyes with me and flexed her gloved fingers indicating I should sit beside her.

"Jimmy, I'm Emma Harkness."

Her voice sounded lower than when she yelled out orders, and she wore heavy make-up. I recalled a movie line about new paint making an old barn look better, but it didn't work for her. She wrote on a tablet while wearing gloves, a strange thing to do, but I wouldn't ask why.

I acted polite, like my parents had taught me, and started the conversation. "You're Miss Harkness, the new radio person, right?"

"I don't want to talk about me, Jimmy. I want to know about your experiences with a Mr. Gaston, a man in a Sterling, Illinois jail. I hear you also know how to make bombs." Miss Harkness waited.

Her bushy brown eyebrows overpowered the gray eyes lodged deep in her face. Eyes usually give away secrets, but not hers, or maybe I couldn't read eyes very well.

"Well, I . . . I don't like talking about him." I stumbled over my words.

"He threatened you, didn't he?" Her eyes never left my face, and her head mirrored my movements.

"He . . . he's, uh, he's in jail."

"Yes, and you're responsible." Miss Harkness kept her unsmiling eyes on me.

For some crazy reason, I remembered a newsreel I'd seen with Billy about a snake charmer playing a flute to control a cobra's movements. Right now, Miss Harkness, with her dead-looking eyes, seemed like a dangerous and poisonous snake. What did the flute player do? How did the snake charmer get the cobra back in the basket?

The charmer made no sudden movements or sounds, and he gradually lowered the flute tip while continuing to play. The snake followed the movement and sound and coiled its body back inside the basket. Soft, gentle words would be my music and my eyes the flute, so I lifted my head and began speaking.

"Mr. Gaston joined the train in California." I moved my head slightly from side to side and let my head move a bit further down with each softly spoken phrase. "He operated the radio. He loved to sing. He directed our chorus. He left the train in Sterling. I'm meeting someone for lunch. Good-bye."

I stood slowly and moved toward the dining car. My raised neck hairs warned me her eyes watched me, and her cold and empty eyes saw me smack into Irish.

"Jimmy, my boy, your choice, apple or banana," Irish said cheerfully and held up his offerings. "Let's eat between the cars, get some fresh air."

Who posed the greater threat, a man with a gun or a woman with lifeless eyes? I followed Irish, and he immediately started another whopper.

"Jimmy, I just remembered a story about a grand fellow from the Emerald Isle named Patrick. A great lad, but down on his luck, and he couldn't even afford a pint. But he had a special gift, the blarney gift. Remind you of anyone you know?"

He nudged me with his elbow and went on with his tale. "Anyway our young Patrick went to

McFarland's Pub and saw every table occupied. But good news, each table had food and drinks a plenty. Here you go, my lad, take the banana."

Standing between cars, the engine's roar and the wheels' clatter almost drowned out his words—almost. He raised his voice so I could hear the story's grand finish.

"Well, our quick-thinking, hungry and thirsty Patrick yelled out that some hay truck turned the corner too fast and dumped its load on a car parked outside. All the diners and drinkers headed for the front door, and our Patrick headed for their tables. He stuffed his pockets with food, grabbed a mug in each hand, and dashed out the back door. God love our Patrick. He ate well that night." Irish laughed heartily at his story.

I didn't join his laughter, because he needed no encouragement in the storytelling department, and I didn't want to be stuck between cars with a man carrying a gun. He could shoot me and throw me off the train, or throw me off without shooting me. If I landed on the ground at this speed, the police would be scraping me up for dog food, if they found me at all.

"Uh, thanks for the banana and the story, but I should be getting back."

"The food may run short, but I'm never short on stories." Irish captured me in a headlock, rubbed my scalp with his knuckles, and pushed me toward the door. "See you later, pal."

After our Ohio stop, I latched on to Mr. Welsh, who had always been kind. He could talk plenty, but his stories had more variety than Irish's and his questions were easier than the ones Emma Harkness asked.

"Jimmy, I had a nice surprise this morning. My secretary and the city manager from Grand Rapids came to Fort Wayne to meet the train."

"I hadn't heard that." My reply sounded idiotic, but Mr. Welsh didn't notice.

"They left home at midnight and got to Fort Wayne at 5:00 a.m. They ran into bad weather and worried about gasoline for the Model A Ford since all stations are closed at night."

"Glad they made it." I offered my second stupid comment.

"I am too, even though they both brought me work. This trip has given me an opportunity to meet lots of mayors and find out how they're tackling problems."

"I guess all cities have problems." I must have been bitten by a "dumb" bug in my sleep, because everything from my mouth today sounded brainless.

"They do. Pittsburgh's David Lawrence is working on cleaning up his city's air."

"That's the city that made steel for the war." Finally, I said something that made sense. Miss Rhodes would be proud of me for remembering that fact about Pittsburgh.

"Yes, but mills also caused problems. Pittsburgh's air is sometimes so smoky that the streetlights are turned on during the day, and office workers carry an extra shirt so they can change at lunch. In Pittsburgh, a crisp white shirt in the morning looks dingy and gray by midday. Mayor Lawrence has an ambitious plan to remove the smoke from the city."

"That's the stuff my teacher, Miss Rhodes, would like in my journal. Do you think Mayor Lawrence would talk to me?"

"He's a politician, Jimmy. My guess is he'll definitely talk." Mr. Welsh chuckled and rested his arm on my shoulder. "Say, I'm getting hungry. You ready to eat?"

"No thanks," I said. "I'll get something later. I'll work on some questions for Mayor Lawrence."

Papa's absence reminded me how much I counted on him, even for company at mealtime. That evening, I ate my grilled cheese and tomato soup with some new guys who'd waved at me to join them when I entered the dining car. They were ordinary men, ex-soldiers, not good guys or bad guys, just normal guys.

I asked them about others who joined the train in Chicago, and they went through the list. The only two they didn't like were Irish and Emma Harkness. Maybe I knew something about judging people's character after all. I'd have to tell Billy.

The drizzling rain and a heavy, smoky smell gave Pittsburgh a dismal feel, but the mayor's smile was sunny. Mayor Lawrence presented five carloads from Pittsburgh, including one contributed by the United Steelworkers Union.

"These carloads of food," Mayor Lawrence told the audience, "are a token of the deep concern the people of Pittsburgh feel for those who are suffering in Europe as an aftermath of the war, a war in which we shared."

When my turn came, I used Mr. Lawrence's idea about the shared war and talked about Johnny and the Deschamps sharing the war and sharing friendship and how we could share by giving food. Afterward, Mr. Welsh introduced me to Mayor Lawrence who kindly answered my questions and explained his plan to eliminate the smoke which choked the city.

I knew I'd get an A on the Pittsburgh story in my journal and scurried back to the train so I could start writing. I included Mayor Lawrence's phrase about the dirty air hampering the city's rebirth. Miss Rhodes would love the expression. I finished my assignment, said a prayer for Papa, recited Psalm 23, and slept peacefully all night.

Samuel's alarm awakened me for Sunday, November 16, Mr. Pearson's weekly broadcast day. Irish either left early or hadn't slept, because his berth showed no signs he'd been there. After the Altoona train ceremonies, I went with Mr. Pearson and a select group, including our Voice of America person, Miss Harkness, to the radio station.

Mr. Pearson entered the broadcasting enclosure which had glass on three sides. I snapped Mr. Pearson's picture in the booth, a gift for Billy's father. The head man at the radio station told us we would be able to hear Mr. Pearson through the speakers, but he couldn't hear us because the booth was soundproofed. The on-air sign glowed.

I remembered all those Sundays our family sat in the living room and listened to Drew Pearson. I knew Martha's family and Billy's family would be listening in California to what Mr. Pearson said today in Altoona, Pennsylvania. Here I stood, watching Drew Pearson do his weekly radio show. I pinched myself, and my fingers left a red mark.

Mr. Pearson arranged his papers, adjusted his necktie, moved the microphone closer, checked the clock and, at the agreed signal, began his fast-paced delivery.

"Good evening, ladies and gentlemen, this is Drew Pearson!

"WASHINGTON – Uncensored diplomatic cables report that the rioting in France and Italy represents a last minute drive by the Communists to take over before American food arrives this winter. The Communists are getting desperate.

"ROME – Italian newspapers are already telling the Italian people the good news of the Friendship Train – describing it as a freewill offering from Americans."

Mr. Pearson talked about several government departments, General MacArthur, and the Marshall

Plan. He asked the Ku Klux Klan's Grand Dragon to dissolve the organization and the Mexican President to return American railroad boxcars. He covered so many topics I couldn't keep up with him, and then came his famous predictions.

Tonight, Mr. Pearson predicted the United Nations would approve dividing Palestine into separate Jewish and Arab states, and that President Truman's message to Congress in special session would denounce business profiteers by bluntly telling Congress we were heading for another depression unless drastic steps were taken to curb prices.

The on-air sign clicked off. I wanted to clap or cheer. I'd seen Mr. Drew Pearson deliver his weekly address to the nation. I'd been on this train with him since November 8, and I'd known who he was—but tonight, I'd actually seen him in action. I knew Drew Pearson—and he knew me!

"Wow! What a swell talk, Mr. Pearson. My family listens to you every week. Billy, he's my best friend, his family listens to you every week too. Thanks for letting me watch. You were great, really great!"

"Not all my listeners are so enthusiastic." He patted me on the back and checked his watch. "Let's get things wrapped up, so we can make our Harrisburg arrival time."

I followed Mr. Pearson, bouncing like my feet were on bedsprings until Emma Harkness fell in step beside me and cupped my elbow like I was her prisoner.

Miss Harkness bent down and whispered, "We'll have time for a nice chat when we get back on the train."

Her words sucked out all my joy and replaced my excitement with dread.

NINETEEN

The firm pressure on my elbow from Miss Harkness propelled me to the dining car and steered me to the inside chair. She sat next to me, blocking my escape, and ordered for us—chicken and dumplings. I don't like dumplings, but I kept my trap shut.

When the waiter stood close enough to hear our words, she asked how we celebrated Thanksgiving and if I'd be home to enjoy the holiday with my sister's family. I ignored her questions about my family and asked where she'd be on Thanksgiving Day.

"My holiday depends on what news I might hear." Her lips turned up at the corners, but the smile never reached her eyes. "The reporters are overdoing Princess Elizabeth and Lieutenant Mountbatten's wedding, when news like this train's success or failure should be covered. The Friendship Train could have been destroyed, if you hadn't interfered. I mean, intervened."

I sampled a dumpling, added salt, tasted a tiny bite, added pepper, and nibbled again. Dumplings taste awful. I chewed slowly, keeping food in my mouth to avoid talking. I toyed with waving my white linen napkin to signal distress. While I played with my food, Miss Harkness finished her meal, slid her chair back, and turned her broad body to face me.

"What led you to name Mr. Gaston? Most responsible adults were amazed at your accusation. They said the man performed admirably at his job and behaved in a helpful and pleasant manner. Now Mr. Gaston serves time in jail because a little boy has a vivid imagination. How old are you?"

I pointed to my full mouth, indicating I couldn't answer.

She continued, speaking softly. "Never mind. Age doesn't matter. Telling lies does. Your father planned the bombing, didn't he? He even taught you how to make bombs. You lied to protect him. People could understand your motive, but you must tell the truth so Mr. Gaston can be released."

I knew her game. We pulled the same stunt in baseball. We taunted the other player, and then he would get mad and swing too hard or miss an easy fielding play because he thought about the ridicule and didn't concentrate on the ball. I fought to keep my temper under control.

If I yelled at her or called her a liar in the busy dining car, people might question my sanity. She'd call me crazy, and adults usually believed grown-ups rather than kids.

"Jimmy, you'd feel better getting the heavy burden off your chest. Your father will understand why you had to testify against him and tell about his horrible plan to destroy the train. Clear your conscience and free an innocent man from jail."

She leaned closer and took my right wrist in her hand, stopping my slow, deliberate eating. Her hand encircled my whole wrist; her hands might be bigger than Papa's. I made my move and nervously stood, but a bit lopsided since she held my right arm on the table.

"Thanks for having dinner with me," I said loudly, the way I talked to Mrs. Martin who never wore her hearing aids. My comment caused other diners to look up from their meals, exactly what I'd hoped. "I'm going to bed early. The Pittsburgh stop last night was a late one. See you tomorrow."

She released my arm, gave a slight nod to compliment my actions, and moved her chair. I wasted no time leaving the dining car. We'd be in New York City on Tuesday, so I only had to dodge Miss Harkness and Irish for two days. After New York, I'd be heading to Illinois to meet Papa, and we'd both go home to California where I'd be normal again.

Normal? Would I ever be a normal kid again? My heart felt full of holes, holes left by Johnny's death, Andrew's death, Mama's death, and seeing Papa shot. Did all adults go around with holes in their hearts? Did they ever get filled with happiness, or did the pain stay forever? Could I be turning into a grown-up? What would Billy say?

I retreated to my berth to think, but Irish waited for me, ready to talk.

"Jimmy, you're turning in early. How about some bedtime stories? I know some corkers about Sean and Mike who lived on a farm with their parents. Now, don't think for a minute that they're not smart fellows, just because they're farmers. No, no, no. These two lads were bright as buttons . . ."

Irish stopped talking and put his inside wrist on my forehead, checking my temperature, the way Mama used to do. "What's wrong? You're not going to lose your dinner, are you?"

"I don't think so." I brushed his hand away. "But those dumplings did not agree with me. Maybe if I'm quiet and still, my stomach will settle down."

I believed my stomach would recover faster if I didn't have to listen to Irish's yarns. They'd become like a toothache, constant and bothersome. The guys I shared dinner with last night laughed about Irish being a big talker, but they didn't share a compartment with him.

"I've got something in my bag to settle a stomach right down," Irish said.

"I probably shouldn't put anything else in my stomach."

I turned my back to Irish. If I took any medicine he prescribed, I might never wake up. Today, between the railroad cars, he could have done away with me, but maybe he'd lost his courage at the last minute. Now the man wanted to give me medicine. Papa's heart had too many holes already. I had to live through the next two days, watch out for bad guys, get Mama's money on its way, try to protect the food on the train, and get back to Papa in one piece.

"You rest," Irish said, giving my shoulder three quick pats, "but yell out if you need anything, and I'll be here faster than a rainbow after a spring shower."

Blessed silence filled the compartment after Irish left. I breathed deeply, trying to inhale the quiet and store its sweetness. The train's repetitive sounds and motions lulled me to an uneasy sleep troubled by nightmares. I woke up three times before sunshine told me Monday morning had arrived.

Today our train would cross paths with the Freedom Train in Harrisburg, Pennsylvania. The Freedom Train carried more than 125 original freedom documents including the Declaration of Independence, the Constitution, and the Emancipation Proclamation. The white Freedom Train with its single red and blue stripes was on the next track. I dressed in record time.

Samuel's smile stretched wider than usual. "Mr. Pearson invited me to go to the Freedom Train," Samuel said. "They close the Freedom Train each Monday for cleaning, but the director invited Mr. Pearson and 20 people from the Friendship Train for a tour."

"Only 20?"

I rushed to find Mr. Pearson, who sat in his usual spot behind his typewriter. Newspapers, telegrams, and typed papers cluttered the table. Miss Canty's hand motion stopped me from interrupting her boss.

"You're on the list, Jimmy." Miss Canty read my mind and heard my growling stomach and added, "Get something to eat. We'll leave in thirty minutes."

Flashbulbs popped and newsmen tried to shoot the two trains side by side, knowing the historic picture might be selected for their newspaper's front page. I snapped train pictures and photographed Mr. Pearson with the Freedom Train director, Mr. O'Brien.

The director explained the priceless documents were in three all-steel cars without windows and each car had special temperature controls. Housed in a new plastic and under glass, the documents would visit all 48 states within the next two years. A 27-member U.S. Marine honor guard accompanied the Freedom Train and one officer guided our tour.

"We take every Monday off, because the days are so long," the smartly dressed marine said. "Yesterday, in Harrisburg, 8,000 people saw the documents. The last man, a Navy veteran, waited in line nine hours for the privilege of seeing the treasures."

"Did the situation in Memphis, Tennessee get resolved?" Mr. Pearson asked the guide, and then explained to us the reason for his question. "The Memphis city government suggested the Freedom Train have separate visiting hours for whites and Negroes, defeating the exhibition's purpose."

"Due to those Jim Crow regulations, our route changed." answered the Marine. "Many fine Memphis people were outraged with their city's decree." He told us about the Freedom Train and the documents and finished by saying "We're closed on Mondays for two purposes—rest and bubblegum removal from the document cars. That job takes two men almost eight hours every Monday. Before you enter, please sign the Freedom Scroll to record your visit, and remember freedom is everybody's job."

Mr. Pearson asked me to tour the cars with him, so I stood next to him as he announced each person's name as an introduction to the officer. I wanted to get inside, but I noticed the officer had put an hand on Mr. Pearson's sleeve to detain him. I should have gone on about my business, but I held back to eavesdrop. My parents told me listening to other people's conversations wasn't polite, but curiosity overcame my good manners. Neither the uniformed man nor Mr. Pearson noticed me.

"Mr. Pearson, your Emma Harkness is not the tiny, feisty, redhead who worked for Voice of America on the Freedom Train for the past month. I guarantee the real Emma is not a person you forget."

"Interesting." Mr. Pearson closed his eyes and squeezed the bridge of his nose before speaking again. "Our Miss Harkness joined us in Chicago. We weren't expecting anyone. The Voice of America man assigned to the Friendship Train took the northerly route and will rejoin us in New York City. This Emma Harkness woman acted so confident we never questioned her credentials." Mr. Pearson gave the marine his truth-demanding look. "You have no doubt the woman you worked with was Emma Harkness?"

"None. We all loved her, and she broke our hearts by telling us she was quitting her job at October's end to get married."

I gasped loudly and the two men looked my way.

"I bet Emma Harkness is in Mr. Gaston's gang," I blurted.

"I thought you'd gone inside," Mr. Pearson said, then turned to the marine. "Jimmy saved our train from sabotage in Sterling, Illinois. He's quite a good detective."

I told the men about Miss Harkness trapping me at dinner and suggesting I confess I'd lied about Mr. Gaston and admit Papa planned the bombing. She told me I put an innocent man in jail. Mr. Pearson raised one eyebrow.

"It's the truth," I said.

The marine offered to send someone to check Emma's compartment and to detain the lady for the police. While he went to get recruits, Mr. Pearson and I joined the others. I sneaked a few glances at Miss Harkness, and then studied the sacred bits of our history.

The Declaration of Independence showed John Hancock's sprawling signature. Our teacher told us Hancock had written his name large enough so King George wouldn't need to use his spectacles. We'd memorized the Preamble to the Constitution in school, but actually seeing the words written with an old quill pen gave me goose bumps. The document cars felt like a church, and we left in a quiet and thoughtful manner. The quiet didn't last long.

"Emma Harkness, or whoever you are, come with me!" A marine officer moved toward Miss Harkness.

His sharp words served like a ready, set, go on a playground and Miss Harkness took off. Women can't run far or fast in high heels, and when the officer reached for her, she formed her gloved hand into a fist, smashed him in the jaw, and took off again. When the marine grabbed her, the navy blue hat with two pheasant feathers flew off her head—and so did her hair!

Without her hat and her hair, Emma Harkness didn't look like a *her* at all, but like a man wearing make-up. We all stared when the marines took our Emma away, and her escorts promised a report before our train left the station. Mr. Pearson herded us past the two trains to the other platform for the Harrisburg boxcar presentation.

My stomach flip-flopped so much that I wondered if anyone could see my shirt moving. The Harrisburg people aimed for five carloads, but presented nine. Dried beans, soap, and macaroni donations kept pouring in from big-hearted Pennsylvanians. Their faces reminded me how good most Americans were. On this journey, I'd seen good faces by the thousands and mean faces by the handful. The good people in our country made me proud and I told our audience how I felt.

Irish appeared at my elbow right after I exited off the platform car. Didn't he ever work?

"Did you hear the one about a man who dressed like a woman in order to get on a train?" Irish raised a black eyebrow and gave me a wink.

"You mean Miss Harkness? What did you hear?"

"I heard she had more in her luggage than clothes. Apparently, our lady planned an explosion in New York City. Once he'd readied the bomb, he'd change into a man's outfit and get off the train. After the big explosion, everyone would be looking for a missing woman, not a man. Pretty clever, huh?"

"I guess so," I said.

"'Twas clever. Our masquerading Emma belonged to Mr. Gaston's group. Gaston learned about the real Emma Harkness quitting her job from this train's Voice of America reporter. They had been chatting about England's royal wedding and Emma's wedding, which was scheduled for the same day, came up. This gave Gaston and his pals two operations—the bombing in Sterling, Illinois and a second attack in New York City. Their Emma joined this train and brought bomb-making supplies with him."

I didn't understand why anyone would deliberately destroy this train and maybe kill good people. Papa's belt filled with Mama's money felt heavy. Before, I'd liked the weight, proof Papa believed in me. Right now, I looked forward to passing this money on to Mr. Pearson. He'd be surprised we

195

had more money for the Deschamps than the amount Papa had given to the French ambassador.

Today had been another crazy day. What would tomorrow, our last day, bring? My steps slowed to match my thoughts, and Irish grabbed my neck from behind.

"Don't think you can get away from me, my laddie." Irish took off his tweed cap and set it on my head at an angle. "I'm your Irish blessing, the friend who's always near you and the one who hopes you'll be in heaven a half hour before the devil knows you're dead."

Dead? Before the devil knows I'm dead? Dead? Good Grief!

TWENTY

Everyone worked two jobs. We prepared for tomorrow's grand celebration in New York City and performed the usual ceremonies when adding more boxcars to the lengthening train. Excitement spewed like the liquid from a shaken-up soda pop. At each train depot, details concerning the salute to the Statue of Liberty, the parade up Broadway, the official ceremonies at City Hall, or the boxcar food unloading and repacking for the sea voyage kept telephone lines humming.

My latest article concerned the Freedom Train documents and the U.S. Marines guarding those treasures. I wrote about Samuel looking at the Emancipation Proclamation and how I felt seeing the actual words written by Thomas Jefferson to declare our independence. I asked Samuel to telegraph my column to my hometown newspaper from Lancaster, Pennsylvania.

I headed for the dining car and guess who waited? Yep, my faithful buddy Irish who requested a table for two and then half-wrestled me down the aisle. His lips started moving before our bottoms touched the chairs at our linen covered table.

"Lucky I caught you before you ate your lunch, huh? Funny I mentioned lucky. You see, I know a lucky Irish lad named Jack, youngest of seven, but he had no quarrel with his place in the family, because being the seventh child, he had more luck than his pals. Now one day . . ."

"Excuse me, but do you know what you're going to order? I think I'll have a BLT and milk." I hated to be rude and interrupt an adult, but Irish would talk nonstop until the train pulled into Philadelphia, and I needed to eat, write in my school journal, and work on my New York City speech.

"You got me. When I start a story, I forget all about eating. What's on the menu?"

During Irish's brief silence, Mr. Pearson joined us.

"Jimmy, I'm working on the final details for tomorrow," Mr. Pearson said. "Would you like to participate in the Statue of Liberty salute? I can arrange for you to be on a tugboat."

"I'd love to do that!" Irish jumped in before I opened my mouth. "Mr. Pearson, you can count on me to keep an eye on this little fellow for you." He reached across the table and rubbed my head with his knuckles, again. How would he like it if somebody did that to him?

"Fine. I'll let the captain know to expect two people." Mr. Pearson jotted notes on his tablet.

"Jimmy, I've assigned you to your own car for the parade up Broadway. Thirty cars will be in the parade and your car is fourth. At City Hall, we're doing a symbolic presentation to France and Italy, so the program may be long, but you're definitely on the list."

"I'll keep my speech short," I said.

"We're expecting 100,000 people for the parade and 25,000 for the City Hall program." Mr. Pearson glanced at the clock. "You'd better order. We'll be in Philadelphia in an hour. They have 20 cars waiting. I'll have Miss Canty give you the details about the tugboat ride."

Before we finished eating, and before Irish finished his fourth story, Miss Canty stopped with instructions for getting to the tugboat and gave me a train ticket to Oakland, California via Sterling, Illinois. She said Samuel would manage my luggage because he'd go to Chicago on the same train. Tomorrow night, my adventure would be finished and I'd be on my way to rejoin Papa. The knowledge made me feel both happy and sad.

After linking the Philadelphia cars to the train, we gathered in the club car and relived the train's whirlwind ten days. Due to the huge crowds expected, I might not see my friends at City Hall, so I snapped everyone's picture. I asked Miss Canty to take my picture, and I made sure she took one with me and Samuel and one with me and Mr. Pearson.

Mr. Guilii, the Italian representative, suggested we conclude our evening by singing the song we'd made up about the Friendship Train. I pulled out my harmonica, and Mr. Welsh, replacing our original choir director, led us. Nobody commented on Mr. Gaston's absence.

The next morning, I awoke to the borrowed alarm clock for the last time, packed my bag, and tidied the compartment. I'd heard Mr. Welsh mention tipping the workers on the train, and I knew Papa would want me to give Samuel something. But how much? And how should I give him the money? If I left cash in the compartment, Irish might think the money belonged to him or me. I couldn't leave the money for Samuel to find on his porter's seat or by his closet, because Samuel's honesty would force him to look for the money's owner. I hoped tipping would be another thing I'd automatically know how to do when I became a grown-up.

I took a crinkled ten dollar bill from Papa's money belt, changed it for a five, put the five back, and got out the ten again. I picked up my Samsonite and searched for Samuel. Ten dollars, ten whole dollars, but the amount felt right, because Samuel had been at my side every time I'd needed help or friendship.

"I'll take your luggage, Mr. Jimmy." Samuel reached for my bag.

"Thanks. Miss Canty said we'd ride the same train to Illinois. I could have gone by myself, but Papa will be glad you're riding with me—for company." I handed him the clock and fumbled on with my planned speech.

"Thanks for letting me use your alarm and for not making fun when I fell asleep in Reno."

Samuel inclined his head. He understood what I meant.

"I, uh, also appreciated the comic books and the wooden nickels. Those wooden nickels actually saved the train, and you gave them to me."

"You're the one who put the pieces together," Samuel said.

"When Papa got shot, I didn't know what to do, and you helped me get to the police station. I don't remember telling you thanks for that."

"You're welcome, Mr. Jimmy. I'll be waiting for you after the speeches."

"I'm glad you like baseball, and uh, I hope Jackie Robinson has a long career." I stuttered, stammered and looked down at my gleaming shoes, shoes Samuel polished every night. "I liked meeting your family, and I hope you'll have a nice Thanksgiving. I hope your four girls all go to college, and have good careers and marry nice men . . ." I rambled, not knowing how to give Samuel the money.

"I hope they will. I'll find you when you leave the stage at City Hall." Samuel lifted my suitcase.

"Wait." I touched Samuel's white starched sleeve. "I know you've watched out for me, especially after Papa got shot. Thank you for everything you've done for me this trip." I held out the ten dollar bill.

Samuel gazed at the money a long time, then bowed his head slightly and accepted the ten. "Serving you on the Friendship Train has been an honor. You're a fine young man."

I turned quickly and walked away, waving at him with the back of my hand. I didn't want Samuel to see my watery eyes.

I found Mr. Pearson in the club car working at his Corona typewriter. He lifted his right hand from the keys and pointed to the bench opposite. He continued working, so I kept quiet.

"The committee debated about having a people's representative on the train," Mr. Pearson said when he stopped typing. "But you've been a wonderful asset. You saved the train from destruction, and your speeches connected with the people. Jimmy, you might be our nation's president one day—but if you are, some good journalist like me will be looking over your shoulder."

"I hope all our presidents will be smarter than I am."

"The smartest people don't necessarily get elected." Mr. Pearson laughed. "You never know what the future has in store. Right now, we have a haberdasher serving in the presidency."

"Mr. Pearson," I needed to get to the reason for my visit. "Papa and I have more money for the Deschamps." I unbuckled the money belt and placed their address and Papa's belt on the table. "Papa gave half of Mama's savings to Ambassador Bonet, and we're giving you the other half. When you meet the Deschamps family, tell them our story, about Mama collecting the money, about her death, about Papa and me being selected for the train, and about Papa getting shot. Oh, you know what to say."

Mr. Pearson put the belt and the address into a briefcase, then leaned his head to the side. "Jimmy, you're aware our trip to France will be during the Christmas holidays."

I nodded. "Sure. The food should arrive in France by December 24. I hope this Christmas will be the best ever for the Deschamps."

"I do too. I'll deliver your mama's money personally." Mr. Pearson extended his hand.

I felt like I'd completed a successful business deal. If I'd been in the movies, I'd have been wearing a nice suit and tie with my hat tilted slightly to one side. I pictured myself looking like Jimmy Stewart, tall, strong, and confident, and not Jimmy Burns, a self-conscious eighth grader.

Irish and I had no trouble following Miss Canty's directions to the tugboat in New York Harbor. Our captain had snow-white hair and his broad ruddy face showed the hours he'd spent facing the sun and the wind. Captain Bill pointed out the other tugboats and the barges loaded with 33 railroad cars set to make the trip around Bedloe's Island where the Statue of Liberty stood. Some railroad cars wore the flags of the United

States, France, and Italy, while other red and yellow boxcars had signs proclaiming Vive la France and Viva l' Italia.

"You may want to stand inside the wheelhouse," said Captain Bill, holding open the door. "Cold wind blowing today."

"I know about cold winds. They say the wind blowing off the Irish Sea can chill you to the bone. One time, a fair girl with the name of Megan . . ."

Irish's words trailed off when he entered the wheelhouse to fill Captain Bill's ears. I stayed outside, turned up my collar, slipped the camera strap over my head, and jammed my hands into my pockets. At some prearranged signal, noise filled New York Harbor. The boats, all sizes and shapes, sounded their whistles, sirens or deep horns. Captain Bill's tugboat chugged forward to move the barges with the symbolic food boxcars toward the Statue of Liberty, a gift to our country from France. The lady with a torch got bigger and bigger. She was gigantic! You can't tell from pictures how big the statue is. Airplanes circled above our heads and fireboats shot enormous water spouts into the air creating rainbows in the morning's sunshine. People on shore threw torn paper pieces into the air, and the scraps danced in the wind. I held my breath like the photographer had said to do, framed my shots, and hoped the tugboat's movement wouldn't make my snapshots too blurry.

I rubbed my hands together, held them over my ears, rubbed them again, and placed them on my face.

Captain Bill knocked on the window and motioned for me to come inside. I shivered and reluctantly opened the door, fearing Irish's never-ending stories would spoil this special moment.

The motor's drone filled the wheelhouse. Irish's mouth was shut. I used my camera to record this rarity. Irish stared at the Statue of Liberty with such reverence he looked like a carving of a pious saint. His gaze never wavered even when I clicked the camera button, so I took a few more shots, then snapped Captain Bill at the wheel. When the tugboat returned to the dock, the captain pointed to a café and told us hot soup and coffee waited for us, with his compliments. I thanked him, and led a silent Irish down the bridge ladder and toward our lunch spot.

Irish sipped the coffee, stirred small whirlpools in his soup, and paused between each spoonful to stare at the statue in the distance. I kept quiet too. When the waiter took our empty bowls, Irish still hadn't spoken a word. I started to worry. *What should I do with him?* The café's aqua-rimmed clock told me I only had one hour before meeting Mr. Pearson for the parade up Broadway. We needed to get going.

"Irish, let's go to our parade spot." I stood and he followed.

Miss Canty had given us maps and directions, but I thought Irish would be leading me. Instead, I compared the map markings to the street names and prayed silently my footsteps would lead us toward the parade's starting point at Bowling Green. I consulted a policeman who confirmed we'd reached the designated spot.

"You okay?" I missed Irish's constant chatter.

"Sure. Old melancholy grabbed me. Me da told me many times about his first sight here, the Statue of Liberty." Irish turned again to look at the lady holding the torch. "My father's family numbered ten, two adults and eight children, but the family only had enough money to send one person to this promised land. They chose me da. He worked hard and sent money for all the family to come to the United States, but the money arrived too late. Only one sister survived those dark starving days in Ireland."

"Sorry." My one word didn't seem enough. I felt ashamed for disliking this man. Maybe Irish's gabbiness hid the painful holes in his heart.

"Da's gone now, his sister too. They both loved America. My father said his proudest moment was seeing his three sons become policemen, taking an oath to protect this great land."

"You're a policeman?" My shock broke Irish's somber mood, and he howled with laughter. I'd worried so much about Mr. Gaston's dangerous friends, I'd forgotten about the detective scheduled to join the train.

"You honestly didn't know? I got the assignment in Sterling, and a scary-looking bald man with a long scar on his face warned me to make certain you stayed safe, or else."

"Mr. Pew. He and Papa are friends," I said. I punched Irish good-naturedly on the arm. This windy November day no longer felt so bitterly cold.

"Let's find your car," Irish said. "Your name and title should be on both sides. You're an important person, you know." He winked. "Say, I've known a few important people . . ."

Irish started another tale, and for the first time, I wanted to listen. He'd finished two hilarious stories by the time we found my spot, fourth car from the front.

"Wave until your arm's ready to fall off." Irish opened my door, then said, "Jimmy, if I don't see you again, I hope you'll be —"

"I hope *you'll* be," I laughed and interrupted him, "in heaven half an hour before the devil knows *you're* dead."

Irish tipped his cap and melted into the cheering crowd. Bands played, confetti fell from the windows like snowflakes, and the parade started up Broadway precisely at noon. I waved at the people lining the sidewalks and at faces pressed against the buildings' windows. My sister had been right. I'd seen America from the Pacific to the Atlantic and not just the land, but the people. I'd only missed two weekly spelling tests at school, but I was different. I wondered if the change showed on the outside. Would Billy notice? Even if he did, he'd still be my friend. I could count on him.

Mr. Pearson taught me to think like a journalist, and I'd learned to look at the people who made up our

207

country differently. I remembered both Johnny and Mr. Gaston fought for our country and our freedom. I learned Mr. Pearson's Quaker beliefs and Mr. Woodall's Mormon beliefs shaped their actions like my Methodist teachings did mine. I admired the war brides' bravery in coming to a new country and realized women like Miss Rhodes and Miss Canty might have to work to support themselves, but they might enjoy working. I knew Samuel and my Papa shared the same type of family connections and dreams.

This ten-day trip showed me I had career options. I could be an accountant, a photographer, a detective, a newscaster, a radio operator, a pilot, or even President of the United States. I could do anything—after being an outfielder for the New York Yankees and setting new batting and fielding records.

I waved at the people lining the parade route, amazed I'd changed so much. Today, I'd speak to 25,000 people without being so scared I wanted to throw up.

At City Hall, Mr. Pearson mentioned programs proposed by the American government, but not enacted, about money going to governmental bigwigs rather than the needy. He promised the Friendship Train food would reach the hungry and said he believed this gesture would promote peace, goodwill and fight communism.

Mr. Warren Austin, the United States delegate to the United Nations, called the train an example of peace mongering and said this generous gift would show Americans were prepared to give help now and in the future as they had in the past.

New York Mayor William O'Dwyer told about the overwhelming response to the train and announced shipping lines were transporting the food over the ocean without charge, the same way the railroads moved the food over the land and never took a penny for doing it. Speakers kept moving toward the podium. Mr. Pearson mentioned many people would speak at City Hall, but he hadn't warned me how long each one would talk. At last, Mr. Pearson called my name and adjusted the microphone for me.

I looked at the crowd, and the love I felt filled all the holes in my heart. I saw the individuals who had filled the boxcars by donating one evaporated milk can, one macaroni package at a time. I remembered the young and old, the wealthy and poor, men and women, all races and religions. The faces looking at me shared my hope, my belief that these Friendship Train gifts represented a love that could unite our world. I stepped to the microphone.

AFTERWORD

The Friendship Train

Post-war America faced many issues: the veterans returning to the work force, a fear of communism, women's new roles, civil rights, and differing opinions about how to get Europe back on its feet. Congress proposed aid for foreign countries, but the debates on implementation methods stalled progress. Drew Pearson, a nationally-known radio broadcaster and syndicated columnist proposed in his October 11, 1947 article that ordinary Americans give needed food to the hungry Europeans. His suggestion met with immediate response.

The original goal, to collect 80 food-filled boxcars exceeded all expectations with over 700 donated. The inaugural train followed the route described in this book, a trip covered extensively by the press and movie makers. This Friendship Train left Los Angeles on November 7 and arrived in New York on November 18, 1947 with approximately ten thousand tons of food. Trains from other areas followed with their donations, and the gifts were repackaged, water sealed and shipped to Europe. The goods arrived in France by Christmas and in Italy by the Day of Epiphany, January 6.

Americans continued to give even after the initial Friendship Train gifts had been distributed. A Library of Congress press release in 1948 cites donations from the New England states to Scotland, mentions California sending canned milk to Greece, and tells about a ship sailing from Seattle with five million pounds of food and clothing for Germany and Austria. Many United States cities adopted sister cities on the other side of the Atlantic, and school children reached out to students in Europe through pen-pal programs — some exchanges started with the letters attached to canned milk or boxes of macaroni. Americans who stood in bread lines and outside soup kitchens during the Great Depression opened their hearts and pantries to Europeans in their time of need.

Train of Gratitude or Merci Train

France responded to the Friendship Train by sending to America gift-laden "40 and 8" boxcars. These boxcars, used for transportation in World War I and II and recognized by American veterans who served in Europe, held either 40 men or 8 horses. France sent 49 of these historic cars, one for each state and one to be shared by Washington D.C. and the territory of Hawaii. Decorated with medallions representing the French provinces, the cars were filled with gifts from the French people to the American people. Presents included wedding gowns, vases, dolls with traditional dress from various regions of France, wine, ash trays decorated with bullet shells, medals won by French soldiers, and personal items. One little boy sent his beloved stuffed dog and a picture of himself—so the doggie wouldn't forget him. Another woman said she had nothing to give, but pressed her finger into the newly-painted boxcar for people in America to see.

States distributed the gifts in different ways. Some auctioned the contents and used the money for special projects, such as education of the children of veterans who died in action. Others used the gifts to raise funds to buy more food to share with the French people. Some states gave the gifts directly to the people of the state, while others preserved the gifts in museums. Today, these historic Merci Cars are maintained in their respective states by either the state government, by military veteran organizations, or by railroad museums.

Nobel Peace Prize

The Quakers received the Nobel Peace Prize in 1947, the same year Quaker activist Drew Pearson organized the Friendship Train. The committee split the award between the Friends Service Council headquartered in England and the American Friends Service Committee. In presenting the award, Nobel Committee Chairman John Gunnar spoke about Quaker work through the centuries. He said the Quakers have shown us it is possible to translate into action what lies deep in the hearts of many: compassion for others and the desire to help them.

In 1948, the Committee for the Nobel Peace Prize issued a statement saying "no living person deserved the award that year." Mahatma Gandhi had been assassinated on January 30, 1948.

Drew Pearson received two nominations in 1949 for his organization of the 1947 Friendship Train, a voluntary relief program for Europe, but did not receive the prestigious award. Pearson, who received many honors during his life, considered the Friendship Train one of his greatest accomplishments.

ACKNOWLEDGEMENTS

The Friendship Train started on a vacation when I read about a "merci car" exhibit. I'd never heard of these railroad gift cars from France and wanted to know the story behind them. When my husband and I returned to Texas, we located the Texas Merci Car and learned that these cars were given in response to the Friendship Train food drive organized by Drew Pearson. The best news was that Drew Pearson's papers were housed in the LBJ Library less than twenty miles from our home.

The act of writing can be lonely, but the writing itself involves the assistance of many helpers. I am very appreciative of those who helped this book transform from idea to reality:

***The research staff at the LBJ Library unearthed the right boxes of Drew Pearson's materials so I could learn more about this gesture of national goodwill.

***My wonderful critique partners, Robert Fears, Chris Lovett, Sharon Lyle, and Karen Swensson offered suggestions, editing help, and the encouragement to continue writing when I felt downhearted.

***Garl B. Latham of Latham Railway Services shared his knowledge of trains and railroading of the 1940's.

***Tammy Brosius provided information about Quaker beliefs and traditions.

***Janet and Ralph Hernandez served as final readers of the manuscript and made revision suggestions.

***My husband, George, for his belief in this project.

ABOUT THE AUTHOR

Linda Baten Johnson grew up in White Deer, a small town in the panhandle of Texas. In second and third grades, she won blue ribbons for her storytelling ability which encouraged her to tell stories for the rest of her life. Linda earned her Master of Arts degree in English and history, worked as a Realtor, a teacher, and logged many volunteer hours, but always followed her passion for telling tales. Her writing credits include fifty readers' theater scripts in addition to magazine and newspaper articles, short stories, and puzzles. Linda and her husband currently live in Frisco, Texas. Extension activities to be used with *The Friendship Train* are available at her website.

www.lindabatenjohnson.com.

Made in the USA
Las Vegas, NV
26 August 2021